The Hanna Gang

Deputy Sheriff Wes Monroe's job was tough, for the sheriff was off sick and a thief was robbing businesses in town. To make matters worse, Jack Thompson, an ex-deputy, was coming back. Thompson had been sweet on Sue Walton, now Monroe's girl, and it was rumoured he had been offered the sheriff's job ahead of Monroe, who was expecting promotion.

When Thompson showed up all hell broke loose, for he was working with the Hanna gang, who planned to rob the bank. With all the odds against him, could Monroe win through or even stay alive? He was destined to face a deadly showdown.

The Hanna Gang

CORBA SUNMAN

A Black Horse Western

ROBERT HALE · LONDON

ISBN 0 7090 7559 6

Robert Hale Limited
Clerkenwell House
Clerkenwell Green
London EC1R 0HT

Typeset by
Derek Doyle & Associates, Liverpool.
Printed and bound in Great Britain by
Antony Rowe Limited, Wiltshire

ONE

It was the early autumn of 1879. Rain was forming puddles in the dust and beating against the huddled buildings in the cow town of Bitter Creek, Montana. Wes Monroe stood in the shadows of the main street under the awning fronting Teague's Saloon, watching the darkened street, his ears strained to pick up unnatural sound. The noise of the driving rain baffled his ears and he had to rely on his eyes to locate trouble before it found him. A stray beam of lamplight glinted on the deputy sheriff's badge pinned to his shirt. He had been keeping a nightly vigil for the past week, hoping to catch Jack Thompson riding into town before anyone else saw the man.

Monroe sighed bitterly. He had no doubt that Thompson would attempt to take up where he had quit three years before. He moved slightly to ease his muscles, and a straying ray of light from a nearby window highlighted his sturdy figure dressed in a rumpled dark-blue store suit. His face, shadowed by the wide brim of his black Stetson, was hard-boned and angular, with a solid chin that had withstood many a heavy fist in a Saturday-night ruckus. There was no sign in his expression of the ingrained toughness the job had bred in him. He was a good lawman, but the fact that minor acts of lawlessness were rife in the town irritated him, for his failure to arrest the culprits made him feel that he was not doing his job properly.

He eased back into the shadows again, his expression softening as his thoughts turned to Sue Walton, who had been Jack Thompson's girl before the ex-deputy had departed abruptly. During the intervening three years, she had turned more and more to Monroe. The news that Thompson was returning had been a great shock, and Monroe was hard put to pinpoint his reaction to it. What he did know was that he would not tolerate Thompson giving Sue the runaround again. The girl had taken a long time to get over her heartbreak, and her gradual movement towards him, although surprising, had filled him with deep pleasure, for Monroe had always cared about her, even when she had been Thompson's girl.

He moved impatiently, wishing he could call in at the dress shop where she was working late, and have a coffee with her.

He forced his thoughts back to the job and all it entailed. A thief was thumbing his nose at the local law department – had carried out a number of minor robberies without leaving a single clue as to his identity. The fact that Sheriff Sam Aitken was too ill to handle his duties had placed the onus of law-dealing firmly upon Monroe's shoulders, for he knew he could not depend on Bill Skinner, the second deputy. Skinner, who was the mayor's favourite nephew, had proved that he could not be relied upon and, when the sheriff finally returned to duty, Monroe intended getting rid of

Aitken's inadequate sidekick. He clenched his hands. There was deep anger inside him, and he knew its existence in his usually placid mind was as a result of that elusive robber, who was goading him with his record of stealing with impunity.

Boots sounded on the boardwalk and Monroe dropped his hand to the butt of the Remington .44 nestling in the cutaway holster on his right hip. He glanced to the left, aware that he was getting nervy, for apart from the ordeal of Jack Thompson's impending return, there was news that a big trail herd, coming up from Texas, was now only two days' ride from town, which meant a heavy weekend ahead, when the drovers reached the grazing ground just outside town and came in for some relaxation.

A figure loomed out of the shadows, a stranger who paused beside Monroe, subjected him to a keen gaze, then peered over the batwings into the saloon.

'You're a stranger in town,' Monroe observed.

'Ain't everybody at some time?' the man replied smoothly. 'Is it any of your business?'

'I make it my business. I'm a deputy sheriff. It's my duty to check all newcomers.'

'Sure.' The man glanced into Monroe's narrowed eyes. 'I didn't see your badge. I'm Link Sullivan. Just rode in and reckon to stay overnight.'

'You got business in town?'

'Nope. Riding through. I wouldn't have come into town if it wasn't raining.'

'Sure.' Monroe's intent gaze had enabled him to judge Sullivan's appearance, and he was satisfied that the newcomer was what he purported to be – a law-abiding man, going about his lawful business. But

Monroe never accepted a man on appearances alone and would keep an eye on Sullivan, just in case.

Sullivan pushed through the batwings then glanced back at Monroe, smiling.

'Would you have a drink with me, Deputy?' He paused. 'I didn't get your name.'

'Wes Monroe. Thanks, but I don't drink on duty. Enjoy your stay in Bitter Creek.'

'Yeah. Anything will be better than a night on the wet trail.'

Monroe returned his attention to the street. There were times when he wished he could be anywhere but Bitter Creek. He had often envied Jack Thompson for the way the man had just upped stakes and quit, although he did not approve of Thompson's methods. He glanced around. The town was secure, although he would make a round later. He turned abruptly and walked along the boardwalk. There was a light in the window of the dress shop and he needed to see Sue, if only to reassure himself of her feelings for him. Jack Thompson had been a pretty big man to live up to.

A big figure, huddled in a slicker against the rain, emerged from an alley and almost collided with Monroe, who stepped aside quickly to avoid contact. Monroe recognized Luke Baine, the undertaker, whose place of business was at the far end of the alley.

'Sorry, Wes, I wasn't looking where I was going.' Baine pulled up the collar of his slicker. 'Is this damned rain ever gonna let up?'

'Don't worry about it, Luke. You been working late?'

'Yeah. Getting a box ready for Mrs Tomlin. Doc says she won't last the night. Are you still on duty? Why don't you let that good-for-nothing Bill Skinner take his turn on night duty? The Council spoke about Skinner last night. They want him out. They don't like throwing away good money, and everybody knows Skinner is useless. He takes advantage of the fact that he's the mayor's nephew.'

'I've been saying that for weeks.' Monroe shrugged. 'But with Sam off sick, there's no one else to do the job, and Skinner is better than no one, bad as he is. Heck, I've spoken to you about it several times over the past weeks, but the Council still haven't done anything. We need another good deputy real urgent, but you'll wait until there's a crisis, and then it'll be too late, which is always how you people work.'

'We haven't needed another deputy since Jack Thompson left. You and the sheriff have handled things pretty good.'

'Sam has been off sick two months now and I don't get paid for the extra work. It's about time I got what I'm worth.'

'We were talking about you last evening.'

'The Council? Sure, that's about all you ever do – *talk*.' Monroe spoke good-naturedly.

'You've got Bitter Creek under tight control. You're doing a good job, Wes.'

'You reckon? Well, I don't think so. I'd like to catch that thief who's thumbing his nose at me.'

'You shouldn't worry about it. Don't take it personal. What he steals don't amount to a hill of beans. The Council think it's someone who acts from weakness rather than malicious intent.'

'So I don't oughta try to arrest him, huh?' Monroe laughed. 'He's committing a crime every time he steals, and has to be stopped.'

'Well, you know your duty better than anyone, I guess. Keep up the good work, Wes, and remember that we all have a cross to bear.'

Baine stepped around Monroe to go on his way, then paused, and Monroe gazed at the man's shadowed face, sensing that Baine had something else on his mind.

'Wes, we've always rubbed along OK, haven't we? In particular, I agree with your tough approach to law-dealing.'

'Sure. What's biting you, Luke?'

'I don't agree with the Council on many things, but we have to go along with the majority. Generally I keep my mouth shut about Council business until they're ready to publish it, but I don't like their attitude about Jack Thompson's return. They're planning to retire Sam Aitken on the grounds of ill health and give Jack the sheriff's badge until an election can be held. I feel you ought to know about that in advance, the way you've handled things around here since Sam fell ill. It's damned deceitful, a slap in the face for you after your good work, and I want you to know that I disapprove of their intention.'

Monroe swallowed hard, his thoughts turning bitter at the news, but he was not surprised. This was just another instance of how Jack Thompson influenced folks with his bluff manner and managed to keep his darker side concealed. It had taken Monroe himself a long time to see through Thompson's projected character and view the real man beneath, but he had never mentioned what he had discovered, for no one would have believed him. They might even have accused him of petty jealousy. Thompson had pulled stakes and left the job, turned his back on Sue without so much as an explanation, and Monroe had been spared the unenviable chore of proving what he suspected, that the popular town hero was nothing more than a cheat at heart, a callous operator who had secretly terrorized a number of women around town for his own selfish motives.

'I'm sorry, Wes.' Baine cut into his thoughts. 'I can see you're shocked, but it would have come as a bigger blow if the Council had its way. Teague, Bentford and Fisher are the big three, as you know, and they ride roughshod over the rest of us when they feel like it.'

'How'd they know Thompson is coming back, Luke? I'd heard about it because Sue had a letter from him and told me. I'm sure she didn't tell anyone else.'

'He wrote to Teague, checking public opinion about his departure three years ago. I think he must have heard that Sam was ill and reckoned to come back as the county sheriff. He always fancied himself in the big saddle, and there's no doubt that if he stood for election there would be a landslide of votes for him. He's got most folks fooled, like he always does.'

'But not you, huh?'

'No. I saw through Jack Thompson a long time ago. I have a grown-up daughter, and what I got out of her after my suspicions were aroused had me reaching for my shotgun. But Thompson was long gone by then, and you can bet that if he comes back I'll be watching him like a hawk. You'd better do the same, Wes. I saw the way Sue was affected by Thompson's departure three years ago. See you around, huh?'

Baine departed, his shoulders hunched against the rain. Monroe shook his head and turned towards the dress shop. He could do with a coffee, and Sue made the best cup of java in town. He tried to lighten his thoughts, but it seemed to him that if Jack Thompson did return then the good days were over and bad times would clamp down upon this God-fearing community he had sworn to protect. He wondered at Sue's feelings for Thompson. Would she go running back to the big trickster upon his return?

The light in the dress shop came from the lamp burning in the back room. The door connecting the shop and back room was open, and Monroe could see through the shop into the little room where Sue did her work of making hats and clothes for the ladies of the town. He raised his hand to knock on the door, but paused when the figure of a man crossed the back room then turned and walked back to the table, out of Monroe's view, where Sue did her work.

Monroe froze in shock, recognizing Jack Thompson instantly. He frowned. How had Thompson got into town without being seen? He stood with his hand upraised, but decided against knocking, a sixth sense warning him to remain unannounced. Sue had always said that if Thompson returned she would not even acknowledge his presence, but here he was pacing her back room as if he owned the place.

Monroe realized that he had stopped breathing in shock, and drew a quick breath. A series of emotions foreign to his nature suddenly arose in his mind, hurting him with their intensity. He clenched his teeth as an unreasoning anger filled him, and went to the dark alley beside the shop. A side window gave a view of the back room and he hurried to it, realizing as he moved, that subconsciously he had always doubted Sue's intentions where Thompson was concerned. He had sensed that if the handsome ex-deputy came back, Sue would welcome him with open arms.

The curtains at the side window were undrawn and Monroe peered into the room. Sue was at the table, her nimble fingers busy with the work that had kept her working late. She was not looking up at Thompson, who was now standing before the table, his hands on his hips as he regarded her. Monroe could hear the sound of Thompson's voice, but was unable to make out what was being said. He took in details of Thompson's appearance, the handsome features that appealed to most women, and decided that the man had apparently done well for himself during the past three years, which did not surprise him unduly, for Thompson had a habit of coming up trumps.

Thompson was dressed in a good store suit. His Stetson was pushed back on his forehead, revealing black hair that was tightly waved. He was taller than Monroe by one inch, but wider across the shoulders and heavier by ten pounds, and he was five years older than Monroe's twenty-seven years. He was still in good shape physically, and his face had lost none of its attractive lines. The lazy, self-assured smile that Monroe remembered so well was still on Thompson's lips, and Monroe resisted the urge to enter the room and wipe it off the big man's leering face. Thompson was wearing a sixgun, butt forward, on his left hip. He was looking as if he hadn't a care in the world.

Monroe gazed at Thompson as if he could not believe his eyes. What had brought him back to Bitter Creek? He had never liked the town, Monroe remembered, for the big ex-deputy had railed incessantly at the petty regulations constricting his sense of freedom. Even Sue had been unable to hold him, her efforts to keep him interested merely pushing his decision to leave into concealment. When he finally made the break, he had departed leaving only a note to mark his passing.

Aware of the misery Sue had suffered for months after Thompson's departure, Monroe experienced a pang of anger and clenched his big hands, fighting against the impulse to enter the shop and hammer Thompson. He drew a deep breath and held it for a moment, mentally counting to ten. Then he reached out and tried the door silently. It was bolted. He paused, wondering what action to take. On the face of it, he had no right to do anything. It was up to Sue to handle this no-good.

Monroe brought his emotions under control and his tension receded. He exhaled deeply, then sucked a steadying breath into his lungs, aware now that he should wait and watch for developments. He could imagine how the town would accept their lawman fighting over a woman. He eased back into the shadows and watched the scene being played in the little room, realizing, by Thompson's manner and expression, that the man was trying to manipulate Sue, as usual.

Rain dripped from the roof of the shop and splattered Monroe's Stetson. He moved back across the alley and stood in the shelter of the store next door, his back to the wall, his eyes fixed on Thompson. He was surprised when the man suddenly nodded, walked to the inner door and departed abruptly. Monroe heard the sound of the bell on the shop door, and then Thompson passed across the mouth of the alley, his boots thudding on the boardwalk.

Monroe looked at Sue, who had not moved from her place and was still stitching methodically, and fought down the impulse to enter the shop and confront the girl, but he shook his head and went to the alley mouth. He would be better employed checking up on Thompson and discovering the reason for the big man's return. Perhaps he could threaten Thompson into leaving again, and staying away.

Thompson went to Teague's Saloon and turned into the alley beside it. By the time Monroe reached the alley, Thompson was entering the saloon by its side door, and complete darkness filled the alley when the door was closed. Frowning, Monroe moved on and looked through the nearest front window into the big room where some twenty townsmen were present. The side door that Thompson had used gave access to the private quarters of the saloon, and Monroe was surprised when Thompson did not put in an appearance in the bar.

A few moments later, Jeff Teague, the proprietor, entered the saloon from the private quarters through a door in the back wall. Tall and powerful, Teague was still a force to be reckoned with, despite the fact that he was over fifty. He was well dressed in a brown store suit, and there was a diamond stick-pin in his cravat. His black hair was heavily greased and set in tight curls that hung over his wide forehead. The main facet of his character was his surly manner, which was not an asset in his business, but did not seem to affect it adversely. His brown eyes were habitually narrowed, as if he were constantly calculating the profit and loss in every situation.

Monroe watched the saloonman. He did not like Teague. There was something in the man's manner, a glint in the dark eyes, the uncompromising line of the thin-lipped mouth, that hinted at unplumbed depths and hidden emotions that were not good. Teague was an inveterate gambler, who spent most of his evenings playing poker with the leading lights of the town – namely members of the Town Council.

Teague crossed to the bar and paused beside the tall, slim figure of Link Sullivan. Monroe narrowed his eyes when Teague tapped the stranger on the shoulder. Sullivan swung round as if he had a guilty conscience, his right hand dropping to the butt of the pistol holstered on his hip, but he relaxed instantly. Teague craned closer to the man and whispered in his ear. Sullivan nodded and went immediately to the door in the back wall. Monroe exhaled deeply when the stranger entered the private quarters and closed the door behind him.

Accustomed as he was to watching attitudes and reading expressions, Monroe was filled with curiosity as he continued to watch Teague. The saloonman looked around the big room, then approached a table where four men were playing poker. Abe Bentford, the president of the Cattleman's Bank, was seated with his back to a wall. His keen gaze lifted to Teague's face as the saloonman approached, and he nodded and smiled, but his eyes returned immediately to his cards. With the banker were Joseph Falz, the storekeeper, Dan Strone, who owned the hotel, and John Kenyon, a lumberman. They had been meeting twice a week in the saloon for as long as Monroe could remember, and all were members of the Town Council. Strone was the current mayor of Bitter Creek.

Monroe moved away from the window. He was more interested in Thompson and the stranger who had gone into the private quarters. He entered the alley and went along to a lighted window next to the door by which Thompson had entered the building. He peered through the window and saw Thompson sitting at a table, with Sullivan seated opposite. Thompson was in the act of pouring whiskey into two glasses, smiling and chatting with Sullivan as if they were friends of long standing. Sullivan picked up one of the glasses and emptied it at a gulp. He spoke, but Monroe could not hear what was said.

What was going on? The question loomed in Monroe's mind. Sullivan, when Monroe challenged him as a stranger, had said he would not have called into town if it hadn't been raining, but apparently he knew Thompson, and Thompson must have been aware of his arrival, for Teague had obviously fetched Sullivan when Thompson entered the private quarters. Monroe strained his ears in an attempt to pick up the conversation, but failed to glean anything that would have helped him understand the situation. The only conclusion he could draw from what he had seen was that Thompson was planning something crooked, which would be normal for him.

Sullivan suddenly got to his feet. He held out his hand and Thompson reached into an inside pocket and produced a wad of notes. Monroe watched intently as a considerable amount of folding money changed hands. Sullivan riffled through the bills, then nodded. He put the money into an inside pocket before turning and leaving the room. Thompson sat back in his seat and drank from his glass, a satisfied smile on his face.

Monroe went back to the street and peered into the saloon. Sullivan was at the bar now, taking another drink. Monroe waited patiently, his curiosity aroused. He stepped back into the cover of the alley when Sullivan turned abruptly to leave.

For a stranger to the town, Sullivan seemed to be

familiar with its layout. He pushed through the batwings and turned left, passing the alley where Monroe was concealed, and strode along the boardwalk as if he knew exactly where he was going. Monroe followed, stepping into the street and moving silently. Sullivan had evidently been paid to do a job, and Monroe wanted to be on hand.

Sullivan went on to the intersection where East Steet joined Main Street. He angled to the right, moving quickly through the shadows into the residential part of town. Monroe followed, eyes strained to mark Sullivan's progress, not liking the thoughts looming in his mind.

Monroe was surprised when Sullivan paused in front of the house where Sheriff Sam Aitken lived. Monroe eased closer, keeping to the shadows, his hand resting on the butt of his holstered .44. Sullivan stood watching the house for some minutes. There was a light in the front downstairs room, and Sullivan went close to the window and tried to peer through the drawn curtains. He failed to see anything and turned to the door. Monroe heard the rasp of metal against leather as the man drew his pistol. Monroe eased closer. The shadows were dense around the door, limiting his vision, but he heard the sound of the door being tried, and it creaked open.

Light shafted from the house, bathing Sullivan in yellow glare. The man stepped over the threshold, gun in hand, and half turned to the door as he began to close it. Monroe drew his gun and went forward.

'Hold it right there, Sullivan!' he rapped. 'Drop your gun. I got you covered.'

Despite his surprise, Sullivan reacted swiftly. He moved to one side of the doorway, his pistol lifting. Monroe fired instantly. Sullivan staggered, dropping his gun as the crash of the shot hammered through the night. Monroe's bullet hit him in the right shoulder. Sullivan jerked and twisted, then fell to the floor. Monroe entered the house to see the sheriff's wife, Martha, sitting at a table, her hands to her face in shock.

'It's all right, Martha.' Monroe picked up Sullivan's discarded gun.

He kept his attention on Sullivan, who was semiconscious, and holstered his gun. He searched Sullivan for other weapons, removing a long-bladed knife from a leather sheath on Sullivan's belt. Then he straightened, his ears ringing from the blast of the shot. He heard Sam Aitken's voice calling from the bedroom and turned to Martha.

'You'd better go tell Sam that some fool fired his gun in the air,' he said. 'Don't tell him about *this*, Martha. I'll come back to you later and we'll talk.'

'What was he going to do?' Martha demanded.

'It's obvious to me what was in his mind, but I'll need to talk to him before jumping to conclusions.'

Monroe bent over Sullivan and grasped him by the left arm, dragging him upright. Sullivan sagged in his grip, but Monroe held him and took him outside.

'I'm bleeding bad,' Sullivan gasped. 'I need a doctor.'

'I'll send for Doc Twitchell when we get to the jail. Where did you meet Thompson?'

'What are you talking about? I don't know anyone called Thompson!'

'So what name *do* you know him by?' Monroe kept a tight grip on his prisoner, although he fancied that Sullivan was in no condition to resist.

'Who you talking about?' Sullivan demanded.

'The man in the back room in the saloon. He gave you a roll of notes. I guess it was to beef Sam Aitken, huh?'

'Who in hell is Sam Aitken? You got me mixed up with some other guy. I ain't been in no back room in the saloon.'

'I was watching Thompson, and saw you take the money from him.'

Monroe paused at the intersection and looked both ways along the main street. Sullivan had been leaning heavily upon him, and now stiffened and turned to fight. Monroe had been expecting such a move, and slammed his right fist in a short arc that crashed his knuckles against Sullivan's jaw. The man dropped instantly, and this time he was senseless. Monroe sighed and dragged Sullivan to his feet, then hoisted the limp body across his shoulder. He continued to the law office and carried his prisoner inside.

Sullivan was regaining his senses as Monroe eased him into a chair. Monroe felt in the man's pockets and removed the bills Thompson had given him.

'I saw Thompson give you this money,' he said harshly. 'So, what gives?'

Sullivan protested strenuously. Monroe picked up the cell keys.

'Come on,' he said. 'We'll find you a bunk to lie on.'

He locked Sullivan in a cell and left the office to confront Thompson, but as he opened the street door, two men lunged in at him from the shadows of the sidewalk, and one of them had a levelled pistol in his hand.

TWO

Monroe fell back under the attack, but before he could resist, the man with the gun struck him on the forehead with the barrel of the weapon. Lights exploded in Monroe's brain, and he fell senseless to the floor. The second man snatched Monroe's pistol from its holster and tossed it aside. Both men entered the office and closed the door.

Coming back to his senses, Monroe found himself lying on the threshold of the office. The street door stood open and rain was splattering over him. His head was aching. He rolled on to his left side and tried to push himself to his feet. At first he could not make it, and sat on the floor, propped up on one trembling arm. By degrees his stability returned and he managed to rise. He tottered to the nearest chair and dropped into it, holding his head in both hands, his eyes closed against the lamplight.

'What's going on here?'

The voice seemed to come from a great distance. Monroe opened his eyes and squinted towards the door. A figure shimmered there, and slowly took on the short, fleshy shape of Doc Twitchell. Monroe tried to get to his feet, and would have fallen if the doctor had not come forward and grasped his arm.

'What happened, Wes? I heard a shot some minutes ago. Were you involved?'

Monroe opened his eyes fully and made an effort to stand unaided. He dropped a hand to his holster, found it empty, and saw his gun lying under the desk. He almost fell over when he bent to retrieve the weapon, and had to lean both hands on the desk and hang his head until a bout of dizziness receded.

'You'd better go to Sam's house and check if Martha is OK, Doc.'

'You look like you need medical attention. There's a bruise coming up on your forehead, which is bleeding. What happened, Wes?'

'Not now, Doc. I've got things to do.'

Monroe staggered towards the cells, and one look was sufficient to see that Sullivan had been released. The cell door stood wide open, mocking him. He turned abruptly, and fell against the doorjamb as his senses whirled. His head cleared slowly and he went back into the office. Doc Twitchell was standing by the desk, his bag open.

'Sit down for a moment and let me examine you, Wes.'

'I've had a prisoner taken out of the cells. I'll come and see you if I think I need treatment, Doc. I've had a bang on the head before. Right now I've got to act fast. Go to Sam's house, like I told you. I stopped someone from killing Sam – leastways, that's what I suspect. He went into Sam's house with a gun in his hand, and turned on me when I challenged him.'

'The hell you say!' Twitchell closed his medical bag

and hurried from the office.

Monroe checked his gun. His fingers trembled as he reloaded an empty chamber in the cylinder. He left the office and walked along the street towards the saloon, reeling slightly. There were men on the boardwalks, all talking about the shot they'd heard, and Monroe ignored them when he was recognized and questioned. He was followed as he continued, and there was excited chatter when his unsteadiness was spotted.

A buzz of speculation filled the saloon when Monroe pushed through the batwings. He looked around, steadying himself. His head was clearing at last. He saw Teague standing by the table where the poker game was being played, and walked towards the man. Teague saw him approaching, and his expression changed when he realized that Monroe was making for him.

'What happened to you, Wes?' Teague asked. 'There's blood on your forehead.'

'I want to talk to you, Jeff,' Monroe said softly.

'Sure. What's on your mind?'

'Not here. Let's go into your private rooms. You've got a lot of explaining to do. I was watching you earlier, and I didn't like what I saw.'

Teague opened his mouth to protest, but the expression on Monroe's face made him change his mind. He turned without comment and led the way to the door in the back wall. Monroe let his hand rest on the butt of his holstered gun, although he was certain that Thompson would be long gone. He followed Teague into the private room where Thompson had been sitting.

'What's this all about?' Teague demanded. 'Why the secrecy?'

'Where's Thompson?'

'Thompson?' Teague shook his head. 'I don't know anyone called Thompson.'

'Jack Thompson. You must remember Jack. He was a deputy sheriff here until three years ago.'

'*That* Thompson. Hell, he ain't been around in three years. Are you sure that knock on the head ain't addled your brains, Wes?'

'Don't play games with me.' Monroe grimaced. 'I ain't in the mood.' He explained the sequence of events he had witnessed. 'That was before I took the crack on the head. So you've got some explaining to do, and if I don't like your answers, I'll throw you in the jail.'

Teague's face had set in a bleak expression which concealed his thoughts. He shook his head. Monroe slid his left foot forward, toes pointing inwards slightly, transferred most of his weight to it, then threw a powerful left hook. His hard knuckles slammed against Teague's chin. The big saloonman staggered backwards, then dropped to the floor. Monroe stood over him.

'Get up,' he rapped. 'It's OK by me if you wanta do this the hard way. I need the truth, and I want it quick. Where is Thompson? Is he still in the saloon? Has he got a room here?'

Teague lay on the floor, staring up at Monroe with fury in his eyes. Blood trickled from his mouth. He pushed himself into a sitting position and wiped his lips on the back of his left hand. The fingers of his right hand lifted to slide under his jacket, and Monroe uttered a curse and kicked sharply at the saloonman's right elbow. Teague's right arm fell helplessly to his side.

24

'I know you carry a hideout gun, Jeff, and I'm ready to go along with that play, if that's what you want. There must be big stakes in this, if you're prepared to try your luck with a gun. So, tell me what's going on.'

'You're crazy! That crack on the head must have twisted your brain. You can't get away with this. You'll lose your job, Monroe. Let's go hear what Harv Fisher has to say about your behaviour.'

'I wouldn't trust that shyster any further than I can throw you.' Monroe dropped a hand to his gun-butt. 'On your feet and start talking. Where is Thompson now?'

Teague shook his head. His eyes were filled with a murderous glint. Monroe bent over the man and relieved him of the hideout gun.

'All right, if this is how you want it.' Monroe motioned for Teague to arise and the saloonman got to his feet. 'You know where the jail is, so head for it, and don't stop for anything in the saloon.'

'You're making a big mistake. Stop this right here and I'll forget you hit me.'

'On your way or I'll hit you again. Don't even think of giving me any trouble or I'll put a slug in you.' Monroe waggled his pistol. 'We'll get at the truth if we have to sit up all night.'

Teague walked into the saloon. Monroe stayed a couple of feet behind the saloonman, gun in hand. They left the saloon together, ignoring the men who questioned them, and went on to the jail. In the law office, Teague sat down beside the desk and made an attempt to ease the situation.

'I don't know where Thompson went to,' he said. 'I haven't done anything wrong. Jack was very popular around here three years ago, and when he turned up earlier this evening and asked to be put up in the saloon for a few days, I saw no reason to deny him. He said he didn't want to be seen around town yet, and I could understand that because he had some trouble with a couple of women before he left the county. But that was none of my business. I guess every man is entitled to make a fool of himself once in a lifetime.

'So, what about Sullivan?'

'Sullivan? Who's he?'

'The man you fetched out of the saloon. He was a stranger, drinking at the bar, and you sent him into the back room to see Thompson.'

'Oh, him. I didn't know what his name was. Jack said he'd met him on the trail and they came into town together. Jack wanted to talk to him. There was nothing in that which was against the law.'

'Thompson gave Sullivan a wad of folding money. Sullivan left the saloon, went along to Sam Aitken's house, and entered with a gun in his hand. When I challenged him, he turned to fight and I shot him. I locked him in the jail and two men took me by surprise, knocked me cold, and busted Sullivan out of the jail.'

'Jeez!' Teague's face lost its colour. He seemed genuinely shocked. 'I don't know anything about that. You're saying that Thompson paid Sullivan to kill Sam Aitken? I can't believe it. Surely you don't think I'm mixed up in anything like that? I swear to God, Wes, I only acted like anyone who knew Jack in the old days would have done. Why would he come back here after three years and pay a stranger to kill the sheriff?'

'I don't know, but I mean to find out.' Monroe picked up the cell keys. 'I'm gonna lock you up now.

I've got a lot to do. I'll get back to you later.'

Teague was locked in a cell, protesting vehemently. He sat down on the bunk, shaking his head as if shocked by Monroe's revelations. Monroe locked the office when he left, and paused on the sidewalk because there was a small crowd of townsmen waiting. He ignored their demands for news.

'Has anyone seen Jack Thompson around this evening?' he asked.

No one had, it seemed, and Monroe pushed through the men and went on along the sidewalk. Rain pattered into his face. He passed the dress shop. Sue was still inside, working, and he hesitated, then decided to put off seeing her because there were more urgent things to be done. He went back to the saloon. There was tension in the smoke-filled room and men were talking about the attempt on the sheriff's life. Silence fell when Monroe appeared, but he ignored everyone, even when Abe Bentford, the banker, called to him.

He went into Teague's private quarters and searched every room, although he did not expect to find Thompson there. The place was deserted, and he left by the side door and walked along the alley to the back lots. Darkness cloaked him and he moved slowly until his eyes became accustomed to the night. When he reached the back lots, he turned right and went to the stable.

A couple of lanterns gave dim light to the interior of the livery barn. Monroe palmed his gun as he entered by the rear door. He stepped to one side of the big doorway and peered around. The place was silent and still, apart from the restless noises of the dozen or so horses in the stalls. He walked around, checking the horses. His own bay gelding whickered softly when he paused beside it, and he patted its velvet-soft nose before going on. He had no idea what he was looking for, but there were no strange horses in the barn and so he went out the front door and back to the main street.

He tried to make sense out of the incidents that had occurred. It was bad enough Jack Thompson returning, but the connection with Sullivan was difficult to understand. Teague had said Thompson and Sullivan had ridden into town together, but although Monroe had been watching for Thompson's arrival, he had failed to spot him despite having seen Sullivan.

He went along to the dress shop and looked in at the side window. Sue was still hard at work, intent upon the fine stitching that had gained her such a good reputation among the ladies of the town. He knocked at the door. Sue started nervously and looked around at the window. She smiled at the sight of his face pressed close to the glass and arose to let him in. Monroe felt sick at heart as he entered, pulling his Stetson low over his forehead as he did so. He was not looking forward to her explanation of Thompson's visit.

'Wes, it's good to see you. I'm just about through for the evening. Would you like a coffee? You're soaked. Why aren't you wearing a slicker?'

Monroe shrugged, waiting for her to talk about Thompson. When she began to make coffee, he felt a dull pang in his chest, for he had expected her to be bursting to tell him the news about the return of the man she had once loved.

'The town seems quiet,' Sue observed.

'So you didn't hear the shot I fired about thirty minutes ago?' he countered.

'Shot? No!' Her face paled as she glanced sharply at him. 'What happened? Were you involved?'

'Naturally.' His lips felt stiff as he spoke. 'I'm the only good lawman around at the moment.'

'Did you shoot someone?'

'Yeah. A stranger. He walked into Sam Aitken's house with a gun in his hand. I figured he was about to shoot Sam, so I shot him first.'

Sue gasped and shook her head, badly shocked by the news. Monroe asked himself why he had not mentioned seeing Thompson in her company. He was disappointed that she had not seen fit to mention Thompson's visit, and wondered why she was reticent about it. He opened his mouth to broach the subject, but words failed him and he decided to wait and see what developed. Sue had to have a reason for not talking about Thompson, and he felt it would be better to try and draw her out on the subject.

He removed his hat and sat down at the table. Sue placed a cup of coffee before him.

'Wes, what happened to your head?' she gasped.

'I was surprised by two men. They knocked me senseless and got away with my prisoner.'

Sue came to examine his forehead, then turned to get a damp cloth to bathe the bruise. 'I bumped into Luke Baine earlier,' he said casually, watching Sue's face intently without appearing to do so. 'He told me Jack Thompson is expected back in town.'

'I know.' Sue looked worried as she turned to him. 'He was here earlier. I thought it was you at the door. I wouldn't have opened it if I'd known it was Jack.'

'What did he want?' Monroe felt relieved that she was not lying about seeing Thompson. 'Did he say why he's come back?'

'He has an urge to see the town and some of his old friends.'

'Did he say anything about his leaving three years ago?'

'I asked him about that. He said he hadn't been ready to settle down and thought I was determined to marry him. He didn't want a scene, so he left without telling me.'

'That's no excuse for the way he treated you. What did you say to that?'

'I told him to leave, that I didn't want to see him again, ever. He just shrugged and went.'

Monroe relaxed while she bathed his forehead, his thoughts running deep. He needed to pick up Thompson, and wondered where the big ex-deputy was holing up.

'You got any idea where Jack could be now?'

Sue shrugged. 'If he doesn't want to be seen, then no one will know where he is. You're not going to make trouble over the way he left me, are you, Wes?'

'No. It goes much deeper than that.' He drank the coffee she had made, then got to his feet. 'I've got things to do. I'll see you home, then go on to Sam's place. Are you ready to leave?'

She nodded. 'I've done enough for today. That dress will be ready when it is needed.'

'You work too hard,' he observed.

'Listen who's talking.' She smiled. 'You're on duty twenty-four hours a day, every day.'

'All that is about to change, according to Luke Baine. He told me the Council plan to retire Sam and put Thompson in his place until an election can be held. That's if Jack wants the job.'

'You're joking! They can't do that to you. It isn't fair after all the time and effort you've put into maintaining the law.'

'They can do what they like, but I've got a feeling that Jack won't fall into line with their plan.'

'Why do you say that? The one thing Jack always wanted was to be the sheriff here.'

'I saw Jack pass some money over to Sullivan – the stranger I shot – and Sullivan went straight round to Sam's house. He would have shot Sam if I hadn't been on hand.'

Sue gazed at him in horror. 'I can't believe that,' she gasped. 'Why would Jack do such a thing? Sam was like a second father to him.'

'That's what I have to find out.' Monroe sighed. 'I'd better be moving. I want to get to Jack before he learns what happened at Sam's house. He might make a try for Sam himself when he hears that Sullivan failed.'

'I'll go home alone,' Sue decided. 'You can't waste time with me. You'd better check with Sam right away.'

Monroe left the shop and went to East Street. He found several townsmen standing outside the sheriff's house, and when they saw him they demanded to be told what had happened. Monroe waved them away and entered the house. He found Martha Aitken sitting in the parlour with Doc Twitchell attending her.

'How's Sam?' Monroe asked.

'We haven't told him what happened.' Martha was a tall, thin woman in her early sixties. She was distressed by what had happened, but her gaze was firm and she looked at Monroe with ageless blue eyes that showed a world of experience in their pale depths. 'I told him

31

what you said to say – that someone fired a gun out in the street. He grumbled that it wouldn't have happened if he'd been on duty.'

Monroe smiled. 'I reckon he's right. I'd like to be able to stick around, just in case, but I've got to try and locate a man. If I put him in jail, then I'm sure nothing else will happen.'

'Don't worry about us.' Martha spoke determinedly, her eyes brightening. 'I can use a pistol good as any man, and if anyone comes around here looking for trouble, I'll be ready to dish it out. I ain't been a sheriff's wife for thirty years without learning how to protect what's mine. Sam taught me to shoot in the old days, when a woman needed a gun to protect herself.'

'I shall be prowling around during the night, keeping an eye on the place,' Monroe told her. 'Don't mistake me for someone else and shoot me, huh?'

'Go on with you,' she replied. 'You know me better than that.'

Monroe departed and stood outside the house for some time, watching the shadows while he tried to decide what to do. He was thankful the townsmen had drifted away. He wanted to pick up Thompson, and wondered where the man had gone after leaving the saloon. The rain had eased slightly and he went back to the main street, intending to carry out his evening round. He avoided the saloon because he did not want to have to answer any questions. He was angry with the Town Council because of what Luke Baine had told him about Thompson being offered the sheriff's badge if he turned up. He had always known that Thompson had been the blue-eyed deputy, and it irritated him because no one had second thoughts for the time and effort he, Monroe, had put into the job.

He checked the business establishments along the west side of the street and returned to the town centre, checking the east side. He paused in the shadows outside Teague's Saloon and peered in through a window. There were no more than eight men inside now, and four of those were the poker-players who formed the backbone of the Council. They were still intent on their game, and he watched them with a jaundiced gaze, wondering what there was about Jack Thompson that appealed to so many.

The sound of breaking glass alerted him and he turned swiftly, canting his head to pick up the direction from whence it came. He looked across the street towards Meeke's gun shop and thought he saw a figure moving in the shadows. He started across the street, gun in hand. If he could catch that thief, it would be something. The man, whoever he was, had always given him the slip, although Monroe had come close to catching him several times.

He reached the opposite sidewalk and stepped into the shadows, looking around while listening intently. The chill breeze blew into his face, making his eyes water, and he gripped his pistol. There was someone standing at the door of the gun shop, and Monroe moved forward slowly, tip-toeing to remain silent. As he passed the alley at the side of the shop, he tensed his muscles, aware that he was making a target of himself. The next instant, a gun muzzle jabbed him in the side and a voice came out of the alley.

'Stand still, unless you're anxious to collect a slug. Get your hands up. You're covered from two sides.'

Monroe dropped his gun and raised his hands,

frowning as he tried to identify the hoarse voice. It belonged to a stranger, and he was certain the town thief was someone he knew well.

'You got sense. Now walk to the gun shop. Someone wants to talk with you.'

Monroe obeyed, albeit unwillingly, but he knew enough about his job not to argue when the odds were against him. The pistol maintained a steady pressure against his left side, and the night was too dark for him to risk attempting to overpower the man. He walked to the door of the gun shop, which was open, and a figure stepped forward out of its dark interior.

'Howdy, Wes. Long time no see.'

'Jack Thompson!' Monroe feigned surprise. 'What are you doing back here?'

'You mean to tell me you hadn't heard I was coming back?'

'Huh!' Monroe uttered a short, bitter laugh. 'I'm the last one in town to hear any news. So, why the return? The last time we talked, you couldn't get far enough away. It's only been three years, so why the change of mind?'

'I heard Sam was gonna retire, and I was promised his job a long time ago. It's something I've always wanted, so here I am.'

'What's so special about the sheriff's job?'

'You don't care that you ain't gonna get it? Heck, I would be madder than a wet hen was I in your boots. That's what I wanta talk to you about, Wes. I saw Sue earlier, and she said she wanted to come back to me if I became the sheriff, but she's scared how you'll react when you hear about it. I said I'd talk to you, make you see sense, because you ain't got no future in this town.

34

The best thing you can do is up stakes and split the breeze. You got no roots put down here, so you can settle somewhere else without trouble.'

'And if I don't?' Monroe was astounded by Thompson's effrontery. He did not believe for a minute that Sue had said she would go back to him. 'You must be loco if you believe what you're saying.'

'You're in the middle of a real mess, but you don't know it, and I'm giving you the easy way out.' Thompson spoke confidently. 'You're a sensible man, Wes, so take my tip. You can't win nohow. Cut your losses and get away from here.'

The smug note in Thompson's voice irritated Monroe. He almost confronted the man with the truth of what he had witnessed earlier, but remained silent, certain that Thompson would kill him in cold blood if he revealed what he knew.

'Are you in love with Sue?' Thompson demanded.

'No. We're friends, that's all.'

Monroe had no intention of answering questions about his personal life while there was a gun stuck in his ribs, and he had no wish to incense Thompson, having had experience of the man's fiery temper. He was wondering what the ex-deputy was doing in the company of several hardcases. Two men had assailed him in the law office, and he was certain they had been working to Thompson's orders. Sullivan himself had been ready to shoot the sheriff for a handful of money. Now there were two hardcases in Thompson's company – he sensed another man on his right – and they were probably the ones who had attacked him at the jail.

'I don't know what to do with you, Wes, and that's a fact. I knew before I returned that you would be a big problem. I can tell that you won't quit. You were always a stubborn cuss, so the sensible thing for me to do is put you out of it. Ike, you and Jake take him out of town and kill him. Bury him somewhere deep, so he can't be found. We got to get this thing moving now, and so far all we've done is waste time.'

Monroe was shocked by the words. He could not believe Thompson would go to such an extreme length to get rid of him. He prepared to fight for his life, but a heavy object crashed against the back of his head and he slid helplessly into a black pit for the second time that evening.

THREE

Thompson stood over Monroe, his pistol pointing at Monroe's head, finger trembling against the trigger. He guessed the true situation that existed between his former colleague and Sue. For several moments he wanted to shoot, but he had a bigger plan to consider and lowered his hammer, then returned the gun to his holster.

'Don't let anyone see you take him out of town, Ike,' he said. 'Follow the trail back to where Mack and the gang are holed up. About three miles out there's a deserted shack with an almighty deep well. Kill this galoot out there and dump him in the well. When you see Mack, tell him to hit the bank here tomorrow morning about 10.30. We made a plan, and we'll stick to it. You got that?'

'Sure thing. We'll take care of it. Have you got the dope on the bank? That's why you came into town. Mack won't like it if you haven't checked it out properly. Remember Cedar Springs?'

'I spoke to someone who is in the know about things around here, and he assured me the job will go off OK. Now get outta here. I still got things to do, and I'm wasting time. Sullivan got off on the wrong foot. I told him what a wildcat this deputy is, and he just laughed, but the first thing he did was get himself shot up. I had to send Pete and Bill into the jail to bust him out.'

Monroe was dragged to his feet and bustled into the nearest alley to be borne away to the stable. Thompson stood for a moment, lost in thought, then sneaked across town, keeping to the dense shadows. He had plenty to do before the Hanna gang rode into town next morning.

When Monroe came back to his senses, he was face down across a saddle, and the jolting motion of the horse as it cantered through the night filled him with a sense of nightmare. His head was aching intolerably. It seemed to be filled with rocks which rolled around painfully inside his skull with every step the horse took. Nausea gripped him. His wrists were tied together, his arms hanging down the side of the horse. He lifted his head to look at his surroundings, and a heavy fist struck him at the nape of the neck. He subsided instantly and listened to the voices of his captors.

'How far have we got to take him outta town?'

'That deserted shack Thompson spoke of is about a mile ahead now,' a rough voice replied. 'That dry well Thompson said to throw him in is on that property, and I reckon he'll never be found.'

'Does it matter if he's found or not?'

'We got to do what Jack says. Step outta line with him, and you could end up in that well yourself.'

'So what's all the fuss about Jack wanting to be county sheriff? We was doin' all right robbin' banks. Sullivan was the wrong guy to send into town to look over the bank, especially with Thompson. Sullivan got mixed up in shooting the sheriff, and this deputy shot him. Sullivan ain't gonna be fit for anything for weeks. Why is Hanna letting Thompson call the shots for the gang? It don't seem right to me.'

Monroe listened, trying to make sense out of what was being said. The only deserted shack he knew was the old Denton place three miles south of Bitter Creek, and his time was getting short if that was where his captors were taking him. He tested his bonds, found them too tight to slip, and relaxed, thankful that his hands had not been tied behind his back.

'There's the shack. Let's get this over with quick. I wanta get back to the gang. Why don't Thompson do his own dirty work? We ain't his slaves.'

'Why don't you ask him when we get back? Or better yet, ask Hanna.'

'Hanna is a wild man. It was all right before Thompson showed up. He's spoiled the deal, him and his fancy ways. So, what does he wanta be a sheriff for?'

The horses halted. Monroe felt himself slipping backwards off the saddle and helped himself down, falling on his feet and dropping flat. Jake cursed and came around the horses to grab him. Monroe lay on his back, bracing his shoulders on the hard ground. He raised his feet and kicked out powerfully, timing his effort. His boots thudded against Jake's stomach with the force of a kicking mule. Jake uttered an agonized cry and went down. Monroe heard a curse from the other man, but paid no heed. He thrust himself up and hurled himself at Jake, reaching for the man's holstered gun.

He was handicapped by having his wrists bound together, but managed to get the fingers of his right hand around the flared butt of Jake's pistol. He jerked the weapon out of the leather and dropped flat, rolling to his right and coming up on one knee, cocking the pistol as he did so. The second man was standing a few feet away, gun in hand, the muzzle held at an angle while he looked for a clear shot.

Monroe fired, and reddish muzzle-flame spurted through the darkness. The crash of the shot blasted through the silence. The standing man fell instantly. Monroe turned to face Jake, catching him in the act of rising with a hastily drawn knife clutched in his right hand.

'Drop it,' Monroe ordered him.

Jake hesitated, then hurled himself forward. Monroe shot him in the chest and rolled aside as the heavy body came crashing to the ground almost atop him. Monroe dropped flat to the ground, his senses whirling. There was a sharp pain in his head. He tried desperately to hold on to his consciousness, but a chasm seemed to open up in his mind and he plunged forward into it. Silence and darkness enveloped him, and he slumped to the ground.

Monroe came back to his senses with a start to find a weak sun shining in a dull sky that was overloaded with heavy black clouds. He was lying on his face on the soaked ground. His clothes were sopping wet and he shivered. For some moments he dared not move his head, but the sound of a horse grazing nearby sent a wave of alarm through him and he finally broke through his inertia and made the effort to move. He raised his head, squinted his eyes against the pain that assailed him, and looked around quickly.

Three horses were grazing within yards of his position, and two men were lying crumpled on the ground where they had fallen in the night. Monroe pushed himself into a sitting position. The gun he had dragged from the man's holster was lying in the grass. He discovered that his arms were numb, the rope around them having pulled tighter because of the rain. He attacked the knots with his teeth, his senses spinning. It took him a long time to make any impression on the rope, but eventually the knots slackened and he freed himself. The effort almost stole his senses again, and he lay back and closed his eyes, suffering untold agonies as blood began to recirculate through his cramped arms.

It was some time before he felt able to get to his feet. There was a crushing pain between his eyes that seemed to anchor him to the wet ground. He managed to get to his hands and knees, his head hanging, eyes closed, and stayed in that position until his senses became steady and the world stopped tilting and swinging. He pushed himself up, his arms trembling, and reeled like a drunk when he managed to stand erect. He staggered towards the nearest horse and clung to the saddle while a spasm of agony rippled through him.

The bad feelings gradually subsided, and he opened his eyes and straightened. He turned slowly to check the two men, and almost overbalanced as he bent over first one and then the other. A bleak sensation invaded his mind when he discovered both were dead. He studied their stiff faces. They were strangers – bank robbers, if the snatch of conversation he had overheard in the night could be believed. He picked up the gun he had used and checked it mechanically, then thrust it into his holster and looked around at his surroundings. The Denton shack was only yards away.

Feeling weak and ill, Monroe forced himself to load the bodies on to two of the horses. He tied their reins to the third horse and swung into the saddle, sitting slumped as he turned the animal towards Bitter Creek. He pictured Jack Thompson in his mind and promised himself an accounting. Whatever his reasons for returning, Thompson would discover that his plans were down in the dust.

By the time he sighted the town, Monroe was feeling slightly better, although his head was sore. He circled the town and rode to the law office across the back lots, leaving the two burdened horses at the rear of the cells. He rode along the alley beside the jail and dismounted at the alley mouth, trailing his reins.

For a moment he stood in cover to look around the street. The town was quiet. People were going about their everyday business. Evidently he had not been missed. He went to the door of the office, pushed it open, and entered quickly.

Joe Parfitt, the jailer, was seated at the desk. Tall and old, Parfitt was dependable and efficient. He got quickly to his feet when he looked up and saw Monroe.

'Wes, where in hell have you been? They've searched the town for you. No one has seen you since last night. Meeke's gun shop was broken into. Say, what happened to your face? Have you been fighting with a grizzly bear? You look like you came off second best.'

'Have you got Jeff Teague behind bars, Joe?'

'Nope. Harvey Fisher was in here first thing this morning. No one knew why you jugged Teague, so Harvey sprung him. Jack Thompson was in here, too. They've made him sheriff. With you gone and Bill Skinner in Helena for a week, there was no one to run the law, so Thompson volunteered to step in. Have you quit?'

'It looks like someone's made that decision for me. But they won't get rid of me that easy. Joe, don't tell anyone I'm back in town. I'm supposed to be dead. Two men I killed last night are face down across their saddles at the back of the jail. They took me outta town to the old Denton place. I'll have to move fast if I'm gonna stop the bad business that's come up. Have you got any idea where Jack Thompson is right now?'

'He's meeting the Town Council this morning. That's where he is right now, I guess. I don't like him, Wes. He's not the type to be a good sheriff.'

'He's not gonna hold that job long,' Monroe replied grimly. 'Let me out the back door, Joe, and keep quiet about seeing me, huh?'

'Sure. Is there anything I can do to help?'

'Not right now. Just carry on as if you haven't seen me, but remember what I've told you.'

'I wish I knew what was going on,' Parfitt muttered. 'When they told me you weren't coming back, I asked for a deputy badge and Thompson said I'm not good enough. He's got some friends coming into town who'll pin on law stars.'

'So, that's his game.' Monroe nodded, putting a hand to his aching head. 'See you later.'

Parfitt acompanied him to the back door, and cursed when he saw the two laden horses.

'Some of Thompson's friends,' Monroe said. 'But these two won't be wearing law badges.'

'And they took you outta town to kill you? What kind of lawmen would *they* have made?'

'Thompson has been riding with a gang of bank

robbers,' Monroe explained. 'I think they're gonna make a try for the bank in town. Keep quiet about this, Joe. Thompson is playing for keeps, so we don't warn him that we know his real business.'

'What about those dead men?'

'Leave them there. I'm gonna have a word with Luke Baine. He'll move them.'

Monroe set out along the rear of the buildings fronting the main street. He reached the back of the bank and hesitated for several moments, wondering if he ought to have a few words with Abe Bentford, but the banker had always seemed to be against him and for Jack Thompson. He went on to the undertaker's yard, keeping cover, and entered to find Luke Baine in the act of taking off his coat. There was a newly made coffin resting on two trestles just inside the wide doorway of the carpenter's shop.

'Wes, where in hell did you come from?' Baine looked around quickly, then went out of the yard to look across the back lots. 'Did anyone see you come in here?'

'No. I was careful. I want to know what's been going on around town, Luke.'

'What happened to you? What kind of trouble did you find?'

'I could do with coffee and food,' Monroe said, 'but I don't want to show myself in town just yet. Were you with the Town Council when Thompson got the sheriff's badge?'

'Yeah. I've just left them. I was the only one to stand out against Thompson getting the job. Sam Aitken says he's coming back on duty, and they can't put anyone in his job unless he says he quits. Then, legally, you should take over.'

'That's why I was taken out of town last night.' Monroe nodded. 'I'm beginning to see the plan now.'

'Come into the house. It's about time I ate, anyway.'

'No. I can't afford the time. I've got to put Thompson behind bars.'

'But he's wearing the sheriff's badge now.'

'That don't cut no ice. I've got a couple of serious charges against him. Any idea where he is now?'

'The leading lights of the Council went with him into Teague's Saloon after they pinned the sheriff's badge on him.'

'I'll spoil their celebration.' Monroe turned on his heel and departed.

'Don't leave me behind,' Baine protested. 'I want to see this.'

Monroe crossed the back lots to the rear of the saloon. He drew the gun on his hip and checked it, reloading empty chambers from the filled loops on his cartridge belt. The door of the saloon opened to his touch and he led the way inside. Raucous laughter and loud voices sounded in the big public room as Monroe entered it. He saw Thompson standing at the bar with the big four of the Town Council – Abe Bentford, Harvey Fisher, Joseph Falz and Dan Strone. Jeff Teague was standing behind the bar, pouring drinks. Monroe went forward, his heels rapping on the wooden floor.

'I'd say this celebration is a mite premature,' he said loudly.

The five men at the bar swung round, the sight of him silencing them. Teague dropped his hands out of sight under the bar.

Monroe grinned. 'I'll kill you, Jeff, if you don't get your hands up. I left you in jail last night, and you're going back there right now.'

Teague brought his hands back into view and raised them shoulder-high.

'Where have you been since last evening?' Bentford demanded. 'We heard you'd quit cold.'

'Ask Thompson.' Monroe's attention was on the big man, who was holding a beer glass in his right hand. 'And while you're at it, you can ask him why he had two men take me out of town last night with orders to kill me and dump my body in the well at the old Denton place.

'The hell you say?' Mayor Dan Strone, who owned the hotel, looked at Monroe in disbelief. 'Have you got those two men to back up your story, Wes?'

'Since when have I needed anyone to back me up?' Monroe smiled. 'I'll answer that question myself, because I can see the way the wind is blowing, but the Council's plans have got a big hole in them. I want Thompson on several charges. I'm arresting him now, and when I've got him and Teague in jail, I'll come back here to talk to you men. Get your hands up, Jack, before you get any wrong ideas. Bill and Ike took me out of town on your orders, and they were so sure they'd do the job, they got a little careless with their talk. I learned that you're running with a gang of bank robbers bossed by an outlaw named Hanna and you're in town to check out the bank for them.'

Thompson put down his glass and turned to face Monroe, his face set in grim lines. For a moment he gazed at Monroe as if gauging his chances, then he sighed and raised his hands.

'You're making a big mistake, Wes,' he said.

'Yeah. I'll sit down and worry about that after I've

46

jailed you. Teague, keep your hands up or I'll shoot you. I might have a little trouble convincing some people that I have a right to kill you, but you'll be dead, and there's no appeal against that condition.'

Teague, whose hands had been easing downwards, thrust them up again.

Monroe moved around the bar and jerked Thompson's pistol from the holster on the man's left hip.

'You won't be in jail long, Jack,' Harvey Fisher said tightly. 'I'll see what I can do when I know what charges are brought against you.'

'You'll need a gun to get these two out of jail,' Monroe promised. 'Come out from behind the bar, Teague. If you've got a hideout gun under your jacket, then you'd best get rid of it now, before an accident happens.'

Teague paused and put his right hand inside his jacket. He drew a small-barrelled .41 pistol from its holster under his armpit and placed it on the bar before emerging from behind the bar. Monroe motioned for him to head for the batwings. The saloon-man did so, and Thompson followed him closely.

'I'll walk with you, Wes.' Luke Baine picked up Teague's gun. 'I wanta know what's going on.'

'Thanks, Luke.' Monroe followed his prisoners and they left the saloon. 'Put your hands down and walk in the street,' he ordered, and they moved off the side-walk, their boots squelching in the mud.

Monroe heaved a sigh as they headed towards the jail. He was feeling far from good. His head was aching and he needed food. They reached the jail without inci-dent, barely attracting attention from the few towns-

47

men along the street. Joe Parfitt opened the door for them as they approached, and grinned at the sight of Thompson under guard.

'Your job didn't last long, Jack, huh?' the jailer commented.

'Get your keys, Joe,' Monroe said. 'Let's put these two where they can't make any more trouble.'

'With pleasure.' Parfitt picked up the cell keys.

Monroe made his prisoners empty their pockets, then put them in separate cells. Teague protested strongly, but Monroe ignored him. Thompson sat down on the bunk in his cell and folded his arms, his gaze detached, a set smile on his lips. He refused to meet Monroe's gaze. Back in the office, Monroe felt his strength ebbing slowly and steeled himself.

'I've got to have some food, or I'm gonna be down on my face,' he said. 'Joe, don't let anyone near those prisoners. If Fisher wants to see Thompson, tell him he can do it when I get back. Luke, will you take care of the two corpses I brought in?'

'Sure thing.' Baine grinned. 'Where are they?'

'Out back. Keep them in your place until I can find out who they are.'

Baine hurried out of the office and Monroe went along to the restaurant. Rain was failing lightly. He slumped into a seat, but a late breakfast restored him somewhat and he finished the meal with two cups of coffee. When he left the restaurant, he was hailed by Doc Twitchell.

'You're a hard man to keep up with,' Twitchell said, 'and it looks like you've had some more bad treatment. How's your head this morning? It's good that bruise has turned out.'

'I got a lump on the back of the head last night,' Monroe said. 'Do you want me, Doc? I'm quite busy this morning.'

'Sam wants to talk to you soon as you can make it. Seems like he was told this morning that he's out of a job because of his illness.'

'They can't do that unless he admits he's not coming back to work.' Monroe shook his head. 'And if I know Sam, he'll be back the minute he feels well enough to buckle on his gunbelt.'

'That's what I want to see you about. Sam is going into the office this morning. I think he can handle it, but he's not to ride, and can do nothing more than sit around the office. Can you help him with that?'

'Sure. I'm missing Sam badly. I'm on my way to see him now. There are some points I need to clear up with him. Are you sure he can manage to sit in the office?'

'I'm not happy about it, but it won't harm him if he takes it easy.'

Monroe nodded and went to the sheriff's house, arriving in time to meet Sam Aitken on the doorstep, taking his leave of Martha. The sheriff, short and in his middle-fifties, was grey-haired and had faded blue eyes. His law badge was pinned to his shirt, and he was wearing a Colt .45 on his right hip.

'Glad to see you up and about, Sam,' Monroe said. 'How you feeling now?'

'A lot better than you're looking,' Aitken responded. 'What's going on? What happened out here last evening? I heard a shot, and Martha gave me guff about some idiot shooting in the air.'

'I'll explain as we walk to the office. First, you better tell me what's been said about you retiring and Jack

49

Thompson taking over as the sheriff.'

'I don't know anything about that.' Aitken shook his head. 'All I heard was that you had disappeared and wasn't coming back, and the Town Council wanted to bring in someone to replace you. Harvey Fisher came and saw me this morning. He told me you had cleared out because Jack Thompson was coming back and Sue preferred Thompson to you. I told him to forget about taking my badge. I'd have to be dead before they could get that off me. It looks like a conspiracy to get Thompson in as the sheriff.'

'I'll be talking to Fisher about that.' Monroe was angered by the rumours. 'There's a conspiracy sure enough, but the Council will have egg on their faces when I've talked to them. Jack Thompson appeared in town last evening. He gave some money to a bank robber by the name of Link Sullivan, who was supposed to shoot you, Sam, only I stopped him. I'll tell you all about it when I get the time. I saw Thompson this morning, wearing a sheriff's badge.'

'I'll take that badge off him when I see him, Wes. I heard a lot about Jack after he disappeared three years ago. He sure ain't the kind of man we figured him to be.'

'I heard about him, but not until after he had gone, and I learned a lot more about him last night. I'll go into details later. All you need to know is that Thompson is working with a gang of bank robbers run by a man named Mack Hanna. They're planning to come here for the bank.'

Monroe went on to explain the rest of it, and saw by the changing expression on Aitken's face that the sheriff was having trouble taking in what was being said. He gave details of being conveyed out of town and what he had overheard before outwitting the two outlaws.

'I can't believe this.' Aitken shook his head. 'Not that I disbelieve you, Wes. But Thompson running around with a gang of bank robbers! I've heard of Mack Hanna. Yeah, there's a wanted dodger on him in the office. Where is Thompson now? He should be behind bars.'

'He is.' Monroe smiled. 'I threw him and Teague in the jail about an hour ago.'

'And I was coming back to the office expecting an easy time.'

'You're gonna have to take it easy, Sam, or else.'

'Or else what?' Aitken chuckled harshly.

'If there's a gang of outlaws with designs on our bank, then you'll have to let me do the dirty work and round them up.'

'Sure. You look like you're doing all right by yourself, if your head can take the punishment, that is. But with Thompson behind bars, the worst might be over.'

'I wouldn't count on that.' A sour note sounded in Monroe's voice. 'I got a nasty feeling the worst is yet to come. We're gonna have to be on our toes. I don't like the way the Town Council have acted. Teague seemed to be on Thompson's side, and Harvey Fisher is keen to get both of them out of jail. The two men I killed last night were outlaws, judging by what they said, and that means the rest of the gang is somewhere around. It ain't gonna be easy, Sam.'

'Abe Bentford is the leader of the Town Council, so let's go along to the bank and throw a scare into him. If he thinks there's a bunch of bank robbers after his cash, he's gonna change his mind pretty quick about getting rid of us.'

They walked to the main street and went to the bank. Townsmen kept coming up to Aitken and enquiring about his health. The sheriff was not looking well. His features were pale and his eyes looked feverish. His hands were trembling, all his movements unsteady.

'Are you sure you should be up and about yet, Sam?' Monroe demanded. 'Heck, your hands are shaking. You're not letting the Town Council force you back to work before you're ready, are you?'

'Nobody is gonna take my job from me,' Aitken replied. 'I'm coming back, and I'll do my duty until I collapse. After that, you can do whatever you think is necessary.'

They entered the bank. Abe Bentford was sitting behind his desk, taciturn, almost sullen, his fleshy face expressionless. Aitken dropped on to the chair beside the desk, and Monroe stood slightly in the rear. Bentford did not seem pleased to see the sheriff. He said nothing, waiting for Aitken to speak, but the sheriff remained silent.

'I heard that you were still too sick to do your job, Sam,' Bentford observed at length. 'When I spoke to Doc Twitchell earlier, he said you'd be off another month at least.'

'So why the hurry to push Jack Thompson into my saddle, Abe? I left Wes in charge, and he is doing a good job, isn't he? How come Jack Thompson got dragged back to fill my boots? Heck, everyone knows he ain't got what it takes to handle the law.'

'He became available, and I went along with the Council when it was decided to give him his chance.'

'But he's *not* available. He's in jail now, facing serious charges.'

Monroe had turned to watch the street, aware that what was passing between the sheriff and the banker was outside his job. He saw three riders suddenly appear before him, coming from out of town. They were strangers, and reined in at the hitching-rail in front of Teague's Saloon opposite, then stepped down from their mounts and stood looking around.

'Sam, take a look at this trio,' Monroe rapped.

Aitken got to his feet and peered out the window.

'They got the look of long riders about them,' Monroe said quietly.

'You're right, and that big guy in front looks like the dodger I got of Mack Hanna.'

'Who's Mack Hanna?' Bentford craned forward to look across the street.

'He runs a gang of bank robbers, and it looks like they've turned up to rob you, Abe.'

Monroe drew his gun, checked it, then returned it to his holster. Aitken put a restraining hand on his arm, shaking his head.

'Don't get off the mark too quick, Wes,' he advised. 'Let *them* make the first move.'

'Sue's just come out of her shop,' Monroe said. 'She's gonna walk through that bunch, and they're looking her over. I can't watch this, Sam. I have to go out there.'

He took off his badge, thrust it into a pocket, then hurried from the bank to intercept Sue, aware that his appearance brought the three outlaws to full alertness.

FOUR

'Hey, Sue!' Monroe called, when he was half-way across the puddled street. 'Hold up there. I wanta talk to you.'

He did not glance at the tough trio standing in front of the saloon, but watched them from a corner of his eye. They had stopped their hand movements towards their guns at the sight of him, but were suspicious, watching him intently. Sue halted and turned to him, only feet from the three strangers. She seemed tense and worried, but smiled as he approached.

'Wes, I've been so concerned about you. Where did you get to last night?'

'Business took me out of town. I haven't been back long. I could do with a cup of your coffee, if you ain't in a hurry.'

'I was about to ask around for you,' she replied. 'Let's go back to the shop and I'll make some coffee.'

Monroe was relieved when she turned to retrace her steps to the shop. The strangers had heard the interchange between them. He did not look around as he fell in beside her, and there was a prickling sensation between his shoulder-blades when he turned his back on the trio.

Sue glanced up at his face as she unlocked the door of the shop. She was frowning. He followed her into the small room which served as the shop. When he closed the door he looked through the big window towards the three men to see that they were entering the saloon, their suspicions temporarily allayed.

'What's wrong, Wes? You're acting strangely this morning. Are you sure that bump on the head isn't affecting you?'

'It's nothing.' He shrugged. 'There's some trouble in town, and nothing will be normal until it's sorted out.'

'Trouble?' Her face showed tension. 'Has it to do with Jack?'

Monroe recalled what Thompson had said in front of the gun shop about Sue being pleased by his return, preferring him to Monroe, but he pushed it to the back of his mind. It was the sort of thing Thompson would say to cause doubt and suspicion and kill trust.

'Jack is in jail,' he said shortly. 'I'll tell you about it later. I wanted you off the street. You may not have noticed the three men in front of the saloon, but they're badmen. I thought you were walking into trouble by passing them, so I headed you off.'

'The town is so quiet these days.' Sue's frown deepened. 'Why on earth have you put Jack in jail?' She paused, looking doubtful. 'Has it anything to do with me?'

'Why should you think that? You know I deal the law according to the book. Jack is in jail because he's broken the law.'

'What has he done? He's only just got back to town.'

'It's a long story. I'll tell you about it later. Right now I have to get back to the bank. I want you to stay in here,

Sue, and don't leave the shop in the next hour.'

He left her and went back across the street, his thoughts bitter. Sue had seemed to be sympathetic towards Thompson, which was galling after the way the man had treated her. Perhaps there was some truth in what Thompson had said. Sue might be harbouring romantic thoughts about him.

The sound of hoofs coming along the street alerted Monroe, and he glanced around as he pushed open the door of the bank. Three riders were coming into town, moving casually, but they looked like long riders. Monroe studied them with alarm flaring in his mind. They were strangers, except for one of them, who was Link Sullivan.

Monroe went into the bank, drawing his gun the instant he was out of sight of the street. Sam Aitken was standing just inside the doorway, his pale face set in a frown.

'There are three more of the gang coming along the street now,' Monroe reported. 'If they're here to hit this place, then we're standing right where we oughta be. We can watch good from this spot. You sure picked the right day to come back to duty, Sam. Are you sure about one of those guys being Mack Hanna?'

'It's him right enough.' Aitken nodded. 'I saw him once over in Helena. Must have been five years ago. They'd arrested him after the Sandy Creek bank robbery, but he escaped from jail before they could hang him. His father, Bud Hanna, used to run the gang, but Mack took over a few years ago. I believe Bud still rides the long trail with the bunch, despite his years. He must be in his sixties now. We'll wait a bit and watch their movements. Stand by that window on the other side of the door, Wes. If they do come in here, we'll have them between us.'

Monroe was grim-faced as he stood to one side of the window and watched the street. The second trio appeared in his line of vision and reined in exactly opposite, beside the horses standing at the hitch rail in front of the saloon. Two of the riders dismounted and stepped on to the sidewalk, trailing their reins, not tying their horses to the rail.

'That guy still in his saddle is Link Sullivan, who was gonna shoot you last night, Sam, Monroe said.

'Well, that settles it, huh?' The sheriff nodded. 'They're up to no good. Let's watch them. They may be here to look over the bank, so we'll give them their chance. The last thing we wanta do is spook them into leaving without tipping their hand.'

Abe Bentford left his desk hurriedly and crossed to the two cashiers. The banker had a short discussion with his employees, and then all three came to where the sheriff was standing. The cashiers were holding shotguns, and Bentford had armed himself with a pistol.

'Feeling different about the law now, Abe?' Aitken asked. 'We got this situation under control, but God knows what would have happened if Thompson had been in charge.'

Monroe saw the banker scowl. He returned his attention to the street and saw the two hardcases on the sidewalk opposite, looking around the street. Both men studied the front of the bank for several moments, chatting casually, but seeming tense. Monroe watched them critically until, after a final look around, they turned and walked into the saloon, leaving Sullivan slumped in his saddle.

'Sullivan can't be feeling too good with a bullet in his shoulder,' Monroe remarked.

'He'll pick up another if they come over here to rob the bank,' Aitken observed.

Two of the strangers emerged from the saloon almost immediately. Monroe tensed, expecting them to cross the street to the bank, but they went to the right along the sidewalk.

'Looks like they're going to the jail,' Aitken said. 'Perhaps they've asked about Thompson and were told he's behind bars. They could be planning to bust him loose.'

'I could leave by the back door and get close to the jail,' Monroe suggested instantly. 'If they are going there, I should be able to catch them in the act. You're well covered here, Sam.'

'That's a good idea.' Aitken looked at Bentford. 'Let Wes out the back door.'

Monroe followed the banker to the back door and departed quickly across the back lots. He ran to the rear of the alley that gave access to the street almost opposite the jail, and made his way along it to the street end. When he peered out of the alley mouth, he looked eagerly for the two men, and was disconcerted when he failed to spot them. Then he noticed one of them standing in the doorway of Falz's general store, watching the street.

The jail was opposite Monroe's position, and he was tempted to cross the street and warn Joe Parfitt, but decided against it because he did not want to scare off the two men. He waited, filled with tension, and heaved a sigh of relief when both men emerged from the store and came on along the opposite sidewalk.

Monroe eased back into the alley. The men reached the law office and turned aside to enter. As the door closed behind them, Monroe left the alley and crossed the street, moving resolutely. He drew his gun, cocked it as he reached the sidewalk, then thrust open the office door with his left hand and stepped inside.

He was in time to see Joe Parfitt falling to the floor. One of the two hardcases was standing over the jailer, his gun uplifted for a second blow. The other was in the act of lifting the bunch of cell keys off a hook on the wall behind the desk. Monroe's abrupt entrance took both men by surprise, and for a few tense seconds they were frozen in shock before they whirled swiftly and tried to bring their guns into action.

Monroe triggered his pistol, moving to his right as he did so to place the nearest man between himself and the second man. The crash of his shot rocked the office. His bullet took the nearest hardcase in the chest. The man rose up on his toes as the .44 slug hit him, then rocked back on his heels before crashing to the floor. His gun flew from his suddenly nerveless hand. Monroe dropped to one knee and a bullet crackled by his left ear. He squinted against the flaring gunsmoke and fired again. The second man pitched sideways, fell upon the desk and then rolled to the floor.

Monroe quickly checked both men. One was dead, the other on the point of coming to the end of his trail. He kicked their discarded guns to one side and bent over Joe Parfitt. The jailer was conscious, his eyes flickering, but he was not aware of his surroundings. Monroe went to the street door and opened it. He risked a glance outside, looking along the street, and saw Mack Hanna and two of his gang standing on the sidewalk in front of the saloon. They were looking towards the jail. He stayed in cover and reloaded his pistol.

When Monroe looked along the street again, he saw the trio crossing to the bank. Sullivan was still sitting on his horse, slumped in the saddle. Monroe glanced back into the office. Parfitt was sitting up now, rubbing his head. Monroe went out and closed the door. He started along the sidewalk at a run, gun in hand, watching the trio going to the bank. When they reached the sidewalk in front of the bank, all three drew their guns and hurried forward.

Shots crashed, and Monroe realized that Aitken had seen the trio draw their guns, and used that as a signal for action. The sheriff fired through the closed door of the bank, and one of the robbers fell over backwards to sprawl off the sidewalk into the street. The other two halted as if they had run into the side of a barn. Monroe ran faster, jumping into the street. He saw Sullivan drawing a pistol, moving awkwardly because of his shoulder wound, but the outlaw was still dangerous, and Monroe fired at him, distracting him.

Monroe triggered shots at the two men in front of the bank, and they turned and ran back across the street to their horses. One of the men fell in the street, then pushed himself up to continue in a shambling run. Monroe fired again, then ducked as Sullivan cut loose at him. The shooting disturbed Sullivan's horse and the animal began to wheel, almost throwing its rider into the street. Sullivan dropped his gun and made a big play of bringing his horse under control. The two men in the street reached their mounts and swung into their saddles. The next instant they were riding hell for leather out of town.

Aitken emerged from the bank and fired at the flee-ing riders. Monroe saw Sullivan, who was the last to leave, sway in his saddle and almost fall, but the man recovered and galloped on out of town. The other two riders had already passed out of sight. The echoes of the shooting faded slowly. Monroe went towards the bank, gun in hand. As he passed the dress shop, he saw Sue's frightened face at the front window and waved reassuringly. She waved in reply.

Abe Bentford was standing beside the sheriff when Monroe reached them. Aitken was grinning, reloading his pistol.

'What happened at the jail?' Aitken demanded.

Monroe explained and the sheriff nodded.

'I'll get along there and check on Joe,' he decided. 'Get your horse and ride out of town, Wes. See which way those fellers rode. I'll gather a posse and send it out after you. It's time Hanna saw the inside of a jail. Take him dead or alive, but don't take any chances with him. He's a dangerous man.'

'Not so fast, Sam,' Monroe responded grimly. 'You're not taking over here. I'll do the running around. Go along to the office, sure, but just sit at the desk. I want a look at that guy who fell off the sidewalk when the shooting started. I'll ride out when I'm good and ready.'

'You're gonna have to follow tracks, and you want 'em fresh,' Aitken responded.

'I can track a fish through water,' Monroe replied with a grin. 'The ground is soft with rain. There'll be plenty of tracks.'

He walked to the fallen robber and bent over the

man, who was lying on his face. The man was alive, but looked hard hit in the chest. Blood was soaking his shirt and jacket. His hat had fallen off his head, and his long white hair was trailing in the mud.

'Heck, this one is old,' Monroe said, and the sheriff came to join him. 'Can it be Mack Hanna's father? They look similar, judging from what I saw of the son.'

'Darned if you ain't right.' Aitken turned to the townsman who was running up. 'Fetch Doc Twitchell, Len. Tell him its urgent.'

'He's coming along the street now,' the man pointed out.

'I need to take a look at the wanted posters before I ride out,' Monroe said. 'I like to know exactly who I'm after.'

The doctor arrived, and dropped to his knees in the mud. Townsmen began to appear. They awaited Twitchell's verdict. Twitchell got up almost immediately.

'Two of you get a door off its hinges and we'll carry him to my office,' he said curtly. 'I might be able to save him.'

'Let me know how you get on, Doc,' Aitken said. 'I don't think we'll need to guard him just now. He looks near dead, and won't be able to make a run for it. I'll send someone over later to stand guard over him, Doc.'

Monroe was already heading towards the law office and Aitken hurried to catch up with him. Joe Parfitt was standing in the doorway of the office, clutching a Winchester.

'I wish you'd told me you were expecting trouble,' he grumbled. 'I took a crack on the head that might have been avoided if I'd known what was going on.'

'Your job is in the jail,' Monroe told him.

'Sure. Well, thanks for walking in and nailing these two. They might have killed me.' He stepped aside to reveal the two bodies lying on the floor.

'Fetch Luke Baine, Joe, and tell him to remove these bodies,' Aitken said.

'I'm sure glad to see you back on duty, Sam,' Parfitt said. 'We might get back to normal now.'

Monroe went to a cupboard and took out a pile of wanted posters. Aitken came to his side and they looked through the dodgers together. The sheriff took five posters from the pile as they came to them.

'This is Mack Hanna,' he said.

Monroe found himself looking at a sullen face and cold, staring eyes. Yellow hair was thick on Mack Hanna's head and face. A long, bulging nose seemed to be stuck haphazardly between the eyes and the mouth, which was thin-lipped and merciless.

'And this is Bud Hanna, Mack's father.'

'They sure look alike.' Monroe laid the posters side by side. 'And it is Bud that the Doc has taken to his office.'

'Yeah. I figured it was. You know what this means, don't you?'

'Tell me,' Monroe said.

'Mack is gonna come back for his father. He'll move heaven and earth to get him free.'

'That's if Bud lives.' Monroe shook his head doubtfully. 'He looked hard hit to me. Doc said he *might* live. We'll have to wait and see.'

'We'll know more about it when we get Doc's report.' Aitken shook his head. 'I want you to go out and see what you can find. The Hanna gang is big. They got all of fifteen men they can call on if they ever need help. Be careful out there, Wes. If they corner you then you'll never see another sunrise.'

'Sure. I'll get moving right away. Tell one of the posse you send after me to collect supplies from the store. We might be out for a few days. You'd better get some special deputies to back you while I am out, huh? The town would be wide open if Hanna came back with the rest of his bunch. You've got plenty of men to call on. And watch out you don't get caught napping here in the jail. It looks like Hanna wants Jack Thompson out of his cell.'

'Don't worry about it. We've got it hog-tied and branded.'

Monroe departed. He went along the street, heading for the stable, and paused in front of the saloon to check on the hoof-prints left in the wet ground. He saddled up and was riding out of town within a few minutes, pushing his horse into a canter and splashing through the puddles. He was able to see the prints left by the riders. A glance over his shoulder showed him townsmen hurrying along the sidewalks towards the bank and the jail.

About a mile out of town, Monroe came upon a horse standing with trailing reins. Its rider, Link Sullivan, was lying on the ground with both arms outstretched. He was dead, his glazed eyes gazing unseeingly at the heavily clouded sky. The outlaw had lost a lot of blood. Monroe got down and checked the body. Sullivan had taken two more slugs.

Monroe threw the body across the saddle of the horse. The other riders had ridden on, probably unaware that Sullivan had cashed in. Six riders came up fast from town, sent by Sam Aitken. They dismounted to view the body, talking excitedly and waving their arms.

'Bill, take this one back to the sheriff,' Monroe said. 'The rest of you, come with me. There are only two of them ahead, and one collected a slug on his way out of town. Sam is sending more men out as soon as they get mounted. Falz is gonna pack supplies and follow us, in case we're out longer than we figure.'

Rafe Orton, the town builder, was a tall, thin man around forty. 'You got any idea who we're after, Wes?'

'Mack Hanna.'

'Never heard of him, but he sure made a mistake riding into Bitter Creek.' Orton grinned. 'Ain't it good to see Sam back on duty? I heard this morning that Jack Thompson was back and figuring to be the sheriff in Sam's place. Is there any truth in that?'

'It don't look to me like Sam has retired,' Monroe countered. 'Let's get moving.'

They rode on, Orton at Monroe's side and the other men following behind. The tracks were plain on the wet ground, but soon rain began to fall in a drizzle, obscuring the distant hills and becoming heavier as they progressed. An hour later, the tracks had disappeared altogether. Monroe shook his head in frustration and reined up. The possemen sat their mounts behind him, not minding the rain.

'It'll be a waste of time going on in this,' Orton declared. 'They could cut off left or right and we'll never find them.'

Monroe considered the situation. He had no intention of giving up before he had exhausted all his options. The lack of tracks would limit him, but he would go on.

'You men can go back to town,' he decided. 'I'll take a look around and swing north to check out P Bar. One of the robbers is wounded. They might have to hole up somewhere close. Tell Sam what I figure on doing.'

The posse turned instantly and began riding back to town. Monroe sat watching them until rain obscured their figures. He shook his reins and continued in the general direction the tracks had been following. Here and there he spotted a recent hoof mark that had not been completely obliterated, and then he hit rocky ground and dismounted to stretch his legs, aware that he was wasting his time and energy by going further.

He left the horse standing with trailing reins, and walked on to check for prints. There was a jumble of rocks just ahead and he walked stiff legged towards them. When he reached the rocks, he stepped into their shelter and saw a number of hoof-prints that the rain had been unable to wash out. Dropping to one knee, he examined the prints, recognizing them. They had been left by one of the mounts that had stood in front of the saloon in town.

The tracks led deeper into the rocks, the prints of two animals showing clearly at times. Monroe went back for his horse and mounted up to continue on the trail. The rain was easing now, and when the tracks veered west and then south, the fact that the wind no longer blew in his face indicated that the robbers were circling and heading back in the general direction of Bitter Creek.

He rode clear of the stretch of rocks and found more prints which were easy to follow. They led into a gully that angled off to the west and inclined towards higher ground which eventually turned into a line of hills.

Looking ahead and trying to gauge the destination of the riders, Monroe felt that they were heading now towards the P Bar ranch, which was owned by Ben Porter. He entered the gully and rode along its length to emerge much higher than when he entered.

The ground was rock-covered and rough. No tracks were in evidence. Monroe stepped down from his saddle and looked around. He moved on twenty yards and then began to walk in a half circle, checking for tracks, his gaze intent as he studied the ground. A rifle cracked and flung a string of echoes across the silent land. Monroe dropped to the ground and rolled into cover. He was untouched by the bullet, and did not hear it pass by.

He removed his hat and raised his head up to look around. He saw nothing and scanned the surrounding area, looking for a tell-tale puff of gunsmoke. There was nothing. Echoes were fading into the illimitable distance, grumbling in the hills. His gaze shifted to where he had left his horse, and a stab of horror pierced him. The animal was down, its legs threshing.

He retraced his steps and was shocked to find the horse dead, shot through the head. He looked around intently, trying to judge the ambusher's position by the way the horse was lying. He recalled the shot. It had been fired from a range of about a hundred yards. He pulled his Winchester from its scabbard, unstrapped the saddlebags, then set out on foot, moving upwards with the lie of the ground, looking for tracks.

Anger bubbled inside him as he looked back to pinpoint the spot where his horse lay. His eyes glinted as he checked his surroundings, his thoughts running deep. Mack Hanna, he mused. The day would come when he would look at the outlaw through gunsmoke, and that knowledge gave him great satisfaction.

He was about three miles from P Bar, and moved forward briskly, wanting to get mounted again and back on Hanna's trail. He had covered barely fifty yards when he heard a horse whicker off to his left, and he dropped into cover, cocking his rifle as he did so. The wind blew into his eyes when he raised up to observe, making them water. He crawled to another position and looked around a rock to see a horse standing only yards away, with trailing reins.

Monroe studied the area for a long time, fearing an ambush, but heard and saw nothing. He began to circle the spot where the horse was standing, ending up behind it without incident. He got to one knee in the cover of a rock and peered around. A man was sprawled on the ground close by the horse, his arms outflung, face upturned. There was no sign of the second man or his horse.

Monroe left his rifle and saddlebags beside a rock and closed in with his pistol drawn. Silence pressed in around him, with only the desolate moaning of the wind in the rocks for company. He reached the horse and patted its neck, his attention on the fallen man, who was dead.

Looking around, Monroe checked for the second man. The dead man was not Mack Hanna, so the gang boss was still at large. There were tracks leading off into the west, and Monroe turned to the waiting horse. Hanna had made a mistake by leaving the animal, but, when he checked it, Monroe found it to be lame in the left foreleg. He stood fuming while trying to work out what to do for the best.

But he had no choice. He needed a horse, and the only place he could get one was P Bar. He led the lame horse and started the long hike to the ranch, his shoulders hunched and his hat pulled low over his eyes to protect them from the chafing wind.

Night was closing in when Monroe sighted P Bar. His legs were aching and he was hungry, but he had not relaxed his vigilance during the passing hours. He sighed with relief as he crossed the yard. Ben Porter was standing on his porch, watching Monroe's approach with interest. The ranch looked deserted in the growing darkness, although there was a glimmer of light showing in the bunkhouse nearby.

'Howdy, Wes! I saw you coming,' Porter called, before Monroe reached him. 'Looks like you got a lame horse there. What brings you this long way from town?'

Monroe sat down on the edge of the porch. His feet were sore. He gave Porter a run-down on what had happened in Bitter Creek. Porter was a short, fleshy man in his middle fifties. His face was the colour of old leather. He cursed fitfully.

'I can lend you a horse,' he offered without hesitation. 'You'll stop for a bite of grub before going on, huh?'

'Thanks, Ben. I'm about caved in, and that's no lie. I reckon to stop overnight and pick up the trail again in the morning, if that's all right with you.'

'Sure thing. Be glad of your company. Leave that horse here, and I'll get Len Craske to take a look at it shortly. Come on in. We was about to eat.'

Monroe needed no second telling, and followed the rancher into the house. Elizabeth Porter, the rancher's wife, was busy in the kitchen, and she greeted Monroe like a long-lost son. He washed up and then sat down at the kitchen table with the two older people.

The meal increased Monroe's feeling of well-being and, when they had eaten, he brought them up to date with the everyday life of Bitter Creek. Full darkness had fallen by the time he followed Porter across to the bunkhouse, where seven cowboys were taking it easy after a hard day's work. Two sat playing cards at the table, another was writing a letter, three were relaxing on their bunks and the seventh was cleaning a Winchester.

Monroe was greeted effusively, and had to repeat the news of the outside world. Frank Carling, who was cleaning the rifle, looked up when Monroe had exhausted his line of talk.

'I spotted strangers up in Aspen Valley two days ago. They was clear of our range, but I didn't like the look of them, so I didn't show myself. There were at least a dozen of them, and they'd made camp and looked like they was staying put for some time. Funny thing was, one of them looked like an old friend of yours, Wes. Jack Thompson. I could have sworn it was him, but he ran out three years ago, didn't he?'

'He showed up in town two days ago and paid a stranger to shoot Sam Aitken,' Monroe said, his thoughts examining his experiences of the day. Mack Hanna could have been heading back to Aspen Valley. 'You reckon there was a dozen of them, Frank?'

'At least. I figured them for a cow outfit, only there weren't no cows around that I could see.'

'Did they see you?'

'Nope. Like I said, I didn't like the look of them. I moved out before they spotted me.'

'Thanks for the information.' Monroe looked at Porter. 'I'll take the horse now, Ben. I better be on the rim of Aspen Valley at sunup.'

'Sure, and Frank can ride with you. It'll save you hunting for that camp. That OK by you, Frank?'

'Yeah. I asked for it. I shoulda kept my trap shut.' Carling grinned good-naturedly. 'I'll be ready to ride by the time you got another horse saddled.'

Porter took a lantern out to the corral and pointed to a good-looking bay. 'That's a good horse, Wes. You wouldn't do no better anywhere. Use it until you can get round to buying a remount. Where's your saddle?'

Monroe explained and the rancher nodded.

'I'll have someone pick up the body and your gear, and send the whole caboodle to Bitter Creek. Will that help you?'

'Sure enough. Thanks, Ben.'

'We got to do what we can to help the law,' Porter said. 'If we don't, we'll be overrun by outfits like that one you're after.'

'Yeah.' Monroe spoke grimly. 'Frank said there were a dozen of them in Aspen Valley. We only saw half that number in town, so I'd better get moving before they pull out and head back to Bitter Creek for another crack at the bank.'

Within minutes, Monroe was saddled and ready to ride. Frank Carling joined him and they set off into the night, heading north. Despite his discomfort, Monroe was filled with excitement. This was a good break, and he meant to make the most of it.

FIVE

Mack Hanna rode into Aspen Valley just after midnight to find the camp-fire low and the rest of his gang snug in their blankets. He reined up and looked around, his mood black. The abortive raid at Bitter Creek had soured him. He blamed Jack Thompson for the fiasco, even though Thompson was behind bars. He looked around for a guard, his narrowed eyes cold and hard. When he failed to spot one, he drew his pistol and fired a shot in the air.

Men sprang out of their blankets, grasping guns and looking around sleepily. Hanna laughed harshly.

'Did you reckon a posse had stumbled in on you?' he demanded. 'Why ain't there someone on watch? You're asking for trouble. You should get a little of what I got in Bitter Creek. They was ready and shot the hell out of us. Thompson wasn't around like he planned. Someone in the saloon said he'd been made the sheriff before we rode in, but he was in jail when we got there, behind bars. We're riding out at dawn, going back to Bitter Creek. Bud got hisself shot. I didn't even get the chance to look at him. They was waiting for us. Thompson has got a lot of explaining to do. Hank, put some life in that fire and cook me some grub. I'm the only one coming back tonight, but tomorrow is gonna be different. The rest of you get back to sleep. It'll likely be a hard day tomorrow.'

The outlaws returned to their blankets. Mack Hanna ate food, although it seemed to stick in his throat. He sat with Hank Farrell, talking about his experiences, going over every little incident that had occurred.

'I got a bad feeling soon as we reached town, Hank. I should have paid heed then. You know what I am for hunches. But Bud talked me out of leaving. Soon as we stood on the sidewalk outside the saloon opposite the bank, I saw that gal Thompson was always talking about – owns the dress shop. She came outta the shop and walked towards us. About the same time, a guy comes outta the bank and crosses the street to the gal. I heard what he said to her. She'd been worried about him. He walked her back to that shop, sees her inside, and a little later he goes back into the bank.'

'Was he the deputy Thompson was always harping on about?' Farrell brushed long, tangled black hair out of his eyes. 'The times Thompson went on about him, I got to know him pretty good. The saloonman, Teague, wrote to Thompson several times, keeping him in the picture about the goings-on in Bitter Creek, and mentioned the deputy getting on close terms with that gal. Thompson didn't like it at all. He has big plans for that gal.'

'Yeah, well, I was for pulling out until we saw Thompson and got the latest news, but Bud insisted on doin' the job. I sent two of the boys along the street to the jail to bust Thompson out, and when I heard a couple of shots I figured they'd done the job, so we started across the street to the bank. We didn't reach the sidewalk over there. All hell broke loose. There were plenty guns inside the bank, and they opened up on us, shooting through the door. Bud was hit first off and fell in the street. It wasn't good, Hank, and someone is gonna pay for that mess.'

'What about Bud? Was he bad hurt?'

'I told you, I don't know. It got so hot in there we had to hightail it, and they shot at us all the time we was getting out of the street.' Hanna stared into the fire, his face set in heavy lines. 'Someone's gonna pay for that, certain sure. We're going back tomorrow and there'll be hell to pay. If Bud is dead, we'll take that town apart board by board.'

Farrell grimaced and got up. He went to his blankets and settled down. Hanna brooded a while longer before unrolling his soogans. Then he turned in and the camp became peaceful although Hanna, tired as he was, could not sleep immediately. He lay staring up at the overcast night sky, making and discarding plans.

Dawn filtered into a sky heavy with black clouds that loaded the wind with tiny droplets of moisture. Monroe crouched on the rim of Aspen Valley. Frank Carling had guided him to this spot before returning to P Bar. The indistinct greyness that had spread over the land was like a cloak, hiding all features. Silence was intense, broken only by the sound of the wind moaning and sighing across the desolate land. Monroe was gripped by a bleakness that chilled him as he waited for daylight to come.

By degrees the night retreated to the west. Monroe did not move a muscle until he was able to see the opposite rim of the valley, then he turned his head slowly, allowing his gaze to check out the great natural depression lying before him. Full daylight was seeping into the rough landscape, chasing out the shadows, but the indistinctness persisted, a pastel grey that made observation difficult. Presently a reddish glow appeared on the eastern horizon and he was able to see to a greater extent. The sun began showing intermittently through the clouds, and disappointment filled him when he saw no sign of the men he sought. The valley was deserted.

Monroe could control his patience no longer. He fetched his horse and rode down into the valley, looking for signs, and found the campsite where a number of men had spent some considerable time, judging by the mess of boot-prints and hoof-prints around the spot where a fire had burned for many days. He could feel heat rising from the ashes and knew he had missed his quarry by no more than an hour or so. The tracks of ten horses led out of the valley, heading south, and Monroe followed them, ignoring the unpleasant conditions, intent only upon tracking down the desperate men he sought.

The land was rough and unbroken. A wide stream meandered out of the valley, flowing south, lined by cottonwoods which clustered along its length. The open spaces on either side of the stream were covered by clumps of sagebrush and greasewood, growing only belly-high to a horse. Monroe could see for miles across the low vegetation.

There were no signs of his quarry except for their tracks. He rode carefully, alert to the danger of ambush. These men were experienced in traversing barren areas and unpopulated ways, and one of them would be watching their backs for pursuit. His thoughts were deep as he maintained all-round vigilance. He did not know for certain if Mack Hanna had joined this bunch, although Frank Carting had said he saw Jack Thompson with them, and Thompson was definitely in with Hanna.

Hours passed monotonously. Monroe wondered where the gang was headed. They were drawing nearer to Bitter Creek, and he became alarmed at the thought that Mack Hanna was making for the town, although it seemed natural that the gang boss would not leave his father behind without making some attempt to free him. Mid-afternoon found Monroe on a ridge over-looking the town, and he reined in and got down from the saddle. He took a pair of field-glasses from a saddle-bag and studied the main street. From where he sat, he could see the tracks he had been following leading down the slope, and spotted where the gang had split into two groups and diverged to ride into town separately, from left and right.

So, Mack Hanna *was* going back to get his father. Monroe had guessed all along that this would be the case. He was about to set off down the slope when he spotted movement at the far end of the street. He turned his glasses on the activity, and tension filled him when he saw ten riders reining up in front of the livery barn. He scanned them intently, and came to the conclusion that they were not Hanna's gang because he could not see Mack Hanna among them. Then he recalled that a trail herd was due to reach Bitter Creek, and studied the faces more closely. The men had the lean, hawk-like look of drovers about them.

He rode down the slope, following the tracks of the riders who had moved in the same direction, angling to the left to bypass the end of the street. He gained the shelter of the back lots on the left and stayed close to the rear of the buildings fronting the street, intending to make an unseen entrance. He reined up at the back of the jail and left the horse standing with trailing reins. The town seemed quiet, despite the fact that Hanna's gang and the drovers were here. He looked around, but saw no sign of the men he had followed from Aspen Valley.

Monroe walked along the alley at the side of the jail and gained the street, where he paused to look around. There was still some activity at the far end of town around the livery barn, where the drovers were, and he slipped out of the alley and hurried into the law office. Sam Aitken was dozing at his desk, but he got to his feet when he saw Monroe standing on the threshold. Aitken was not looking well. His face was ashen, his breathing harsh, and he moved with difficulty, but grinned at Monroe.

'Glad to see you back, Wes. How'd you get on?'

Monroe related his experiences and saw the lines deepen on Aitken's face.

'So, the gang is back, huh? That's bad. I got word earlier that the herd we been expecting is just outside of town and the drovers will be in any time. If the gang mixes in with the drovers, then we're gonna have our work cut out. The only face I know in that crooked bunch is Mack Hanna's, and you can bet he won't show himself around.'

'I saw the drovers riding into the livery barn as I came in.' Monroe sighed. 'What else has been happening? Tell me about Bud Hanna.'

'He'll live, Doc says, but it will be a fight to save him. Bud's age is against him. Mack Hanna wouldn't be able to move him inside of a week, because to do so would kill him for sure. We got to get after the gang, Wes, and pull them in. I know a lot about Mack Hanna. He's mean right through to the spine. I heard he's got a kink in his brain. The slightest thing can trigger him into a frenzy, and in that frame of mind he's likely to go on a killing spree.'

'I didn't get a look at any of the gang. I followed their tracks all the way from Aspen Valley and didn't see hide nor hair of them.'

'We know what Mack Hanna looks like, so all we got to do is watch him and those he mixes with.'

'I'll make a round of the town shortly.' Monroe sat down on a corner of the desk. 'Have you still got Thompson and Teague in the cells?'

The sheriff nodded. 'I've had a couple of sessions with Jack, but he ain't giving anything away. He denies paying Sullivan to kill me – reckons you're lying about that because you want him out of the way, which would leave you with a clear field around Sue. Teague denies all knowledge of any plot to kill me and claims he's innocent. Harvey Fisher has been in a couple of times, trying to get Teague out on bail. I told him to wait until you showed up.'

'I need to get cleaned up and feed myself before doing anything else.' Monroe stood up. 'I'll put my horse in the barn and then get back into the old routine, huh?'

'I'm hanging on in here by the skin of my teeth,' Aitken admitted. 'I feel like all hell, but I won't give in.

I can sit here in the office, but anything more will put me on my back.'

'Now you know why I've been carping on about having extra help in the law department.' Monroe frowned. 'We need a couple of extra deputies, especially right now. What would you do if Mack Hanna suddenly walked in here with a couple of his gang and threw down on you? He'd have Thompson out of his cell easy as hooking fish in a barrel.'

'You don't have to tell me,' Aitken said grimly. 'I've managed to convince Tom Parke and Frank Hallam to act as special deputies until this is settled. Abe Bentford didn't think much of it when I told him – the council have always been tight where money is concerned – but he shut up when I spelled out the alternatve. He's afraid the bank will be hit again.'

'So, what do you reckon Hanna will do when he learns that Bud won't be fit to travel inside of a week?'

'If he's got any sense, he'll pull out until his old man can sit on a horse.' Aitken spoke through clenched teeth. 'If Bud dies in the mean time, then we can expect bad trouble. I shot Bud, and Mack will want my hide in payment, and a few more just for the hell of it. That's what he did over in Greasewood a few years ago. His brother was killed that time, and Mack blew his top and went through the town. He killed the sheriff, two deputies, and several of the townsfolk, including a woman and a child.'

'I'll take a turn around the town,' Monroe decided. 'I'll need to talk to the drovers, remind them of the law we got against them carrying guns inside of town limits. We don't want any trouble from them. If I see Hanna, I'll check who he associates with. It would help if we knew the gang by sight.' He paused as a thought struck him. 'On second thoughts, I could have a few words with Thompson. I might get something out of him.'

He picked up the cell keys and let himself through the door closing off the cell block from the office. Teague, in the nearest cell, was lying on his bunk, trying to sleep. Jack Thompson was in a cell at the far end of the passage. Monroe walked to the door of the cell and stood with folded arms. Thompson was lounging on his bunk, hands behind his head. His expression was hard, and did not change when he saw Monroe.

'What happened to you, Jack?' Monroe demanded. 'You were always full of big ideas. I remember you saying you were gonna set the world alight. So what went wrong? You left us without telling a soul what was in your mind, and you're back after three years in the company of the worst gang of robbers that ever hit a bank. You've done nothing but lie and cheat.'

'You seem to have all the answers, Wes, so don't bother me. I got nothing to say to you.' Thompson smiled and closed his eyes.

Monroe gazed at the man. Thompson snored mockingly. Monroe turned on his heel to depart and heard Thompson chuckle quietly. Monroe paused.

'My day will come, Jack,' he promised. 'You're up to your eyes in this, and you're gonna be sorry you decided to come back.'

'You're gonna be even sorrier I did,' Thompson responded.

Monroe left the office and fetched his horse. He mounted and rode along the back lots to the stable to find all the stalls occupied. He took the horse through to the front yard and allowed the animal to drink its fill from the water trough. When he led it back inside the barn, Fred Barlow, the liveryman, emerged from his office.

'Howdy, Wes. I ain't got a spare stall in the place.' A grin of satisfaction was showing on the ostler's thin face. Barlow was in his sixties, stoop-shouldered, and looked as if a strong wind could blow him over. 'I'm having to put nags into Murphy's barn out back. That herd from Texas is being held just out of town and most of the drovers have come in for a few drinks. They been on the trail for months.' He paused, his dark eyes narrowed. 'You ain't gonna give them trouble, are you, Wes? We can do with the money they'll spend in town, so don't chase them off if they get a bit rowdy.'

'I saw them ride in.' Monroe suppressed a sigh. 'I won't bother them if they don't cause any trouble, but I ain't optimistic. You know what drovers are like at the end of a trail. Has another group of riders showed up – say, ten riders?'

'Strangers?'

'That's right.'

Barlow shook his head. 'Ain't seen strangers since the bank robbers rode in yesterday. You ain't expecting them back, are you? I reckon you did pretty good with them, Wes. I hear the old man who was shot is like to die.'

'Doc Twitchell will save him if he can, I guess.' Wes led his mount to the back door. 'I had to borrow this horse from Ben Porter. Mack Hanna killed mine. I'll put this one in Murphy's barn.'

'I'll take care of it in a moment,' Barlow said.

Monroe wondered about the ten horses he had trailed from Aspen Valley. Where were they? He led the horse into the barn behind the stable and took care of it. He looked around the back lots, but saw no sign of horses. It was as if the outlaws had vanished into thin air, but he had expected Mack Hanna to play it cool. The gang boss would want to learn of the situation around town before taking any action, having to stay undercover because he could be recognized.

The faint rustle of a furtive boot moving through straw cut through Monroe's thoughts, alerting him to his surroundings. He stepped forward one pace and turned quickly, left arm lifting to act as a bar, and side-stepped a big figure bearing down on him. He saw a knife in the man's right hand, sweeping in a deadly arc to connect with his body, and pushed his left arm forward and upward to meet the blow. The descending arm thudded against his defensive block, and he reached up with his right hand and seized hold of the man's wrist, twisting it powerfully. The man uttered a hoarse cry as his arm was forced behind him and held in a painful, unbreakable grip.

Monroe changed hands quickly and smoothly. His left gripped the man's wrist while his right snatched the knife from the man's loosening grasp. He threw the lethal blade out through the doorway, then dropped his right hand to his holstered pistol. The weapon rasped clear of its leather and swung quickly, the movement ending with a sullen thud when the barrel connected with the man's skull. Monroe straightened and stepped back as the man collapsed into the straw.

He looked around for more trouble, but the barn appeared to be deserted now. He peered down into the bearded face of the stranger, and bent to pull a pistol out of the man's holster. The man was stirring, and opened his eyes presently. He pushed himself into a sitting position, rubbing his head where Monroe's pistol barrel had caught him. Then he became aware of Monroe standing before him, and froze, his eyes filling with wariness.

'Get up,' Monroe ordered him. 'What's your name? Are you a drover, or one of Mack Hanna's men?'

The man scrambled to his feet and stood shaking his head. Monroe remained just out of arm's length, his pistol lined up on the man's body.

'I'm sorry,' the man replied. 'I thought you was someone else. You ain't the man I'm looking for.'

Monroe grinned. 'You'll have to do better'n that. I reckon you saw my law badge and it triggered you off. What's your name?'

'Jake Wells.'

'You're a stranger in town, so tell me about yourself.'

'I'm riding through. I thought you were someone I'd had trouble with on the trail.'

Monroe waggled his gun. 'I ain't got time for this. Come on. I'll put you in the jail until you can remember who you are and what you're doing in Bitter Creek.'

Wells walked out of the barn, but swung suddenly as he passed Monroe, his right hand clenching into a fist and speeding toward Monroe's jaw. Monroe grinned and swayed back on his heels, letting the blow pass his chin. He leaned forward, his feet changing position, and his left fist smacked solidly against Wells's chin. He shook his head as the man fell to the ground.

'Quit fooling around,' he rasped. 'Get up and head to the left. You're going to jail.'

Wells staggered to his feet, shaking his head, and seemed to have had the fight knocked out of him. He shambled along, shaking his head repeatedly, and Monroe followed him, watching his surroundings, wondering where Hanna and his bunch had concealed themselves.

Sam Aitken got to his feet when Monroe ushered his prisoner into the office, reaching for the cell keys as he did so. Monroe explained the incident, and they put Wells in a cell.

'I'll come back after I've eaten,' Monroe said. 'I've got to have some food.

'He'll be here when you get back.' Aitken grinned, although his face was showing weariness. 'Looks like the trouble is starting, huh?'

'The trouble is that we don't know drovers from outlaws,' Monroe countered. 'I'll check them out after I've eaten, if they'll give me a few minutes to myself. I don't expect them to be reasonable, but we'll see.'

He shook his head ruefully and left the office, passing the dress shop without a glance inside for Sue, and went along to the restaurant, where he ordered a meal. Waiting for it to be served, he went to the rear door to check the back lots on that side of the street. He saw no horses out back, and frowned as he moved back to his table and sat down to eat. The restaurant was crowded more than usual, and he guessed that some of the diners present were either drovers from the herd or even some of the outlaws. He looked around, unable to tell who was law-abiding and who was not. The only thing he did know was that Mack Hanna was not present.

He felt ready to resume his duties when he had finished the meal. He removed his law star from his vest, aware that it would attract all the wrong attention, and went along the street to the doctor's house, to find Twitchell in his office, treating a patient. When they were alone, he enquired after Bud Hanna.

The doctor frowned and shook his head. 'It's touch and go with him, Wes. He ain't out of the wood yet, not by a long rope, but I think he will make it if he gets plenty of rest and attention.'

'Can he be moved, Doc?'

'Sure, if you want to kill him. Where do you want to take him, for God's sake?'

'To the jail.'

'There's no need to put him behind bars. He ain't going anywhere for a long time. If you leave him here, he might tempt the rest of his bunch to come in and get him, and you could clean up on them.'

'There's no "might" about it.' Monroe grimaced. 'The gang is in town. The trouble is, so are about ten drovers from that herd we've been expecting to show up, and we can't tell the difference between drovers and robbers. I'm on my way to look up the drovers. It'll help if we can get them out of town for a spell. That way we'd be able to round up any other strangers.'

'This is the helluva note,' Twitchell muttered. 'The gang will learn Bud is here, and I'll be knee-deep in badmen. I'll have to get Mattie away from here. Excuse me, Wes.'

Twitchell left the office and Monroe heard him calling for his wife. Minutes passed, and when Twitchell returned he seemed angry.

'That wife of mine hasn't listened to reason in thirty years of marriage,' he complained. 'And she's still riding the same trail. She refuses to leave.'

'It would be safer for all concerned if Bud Hanna was

behind bars. When it gets dark I'll bring a couple of men with a stretcher. We'll be careful with Hanna, and take him to the jail. That will direct the attention of the gang to us rather than you. Make no mistake about it, Doc, if Mack Hanna comes here for his pa, then he'll likely cut you down, and your wife. He's that kind of a man. From what I've heard tell about him, he's a mad dog. We've got to protect the town and everyone in it, and that includes you, Doc.'

'Come and see me later and I'll reassess Hanna's chances. But he stays here if I think it's too dangerous to move him.'

'It'll be too dangerous for you and the rest of the town if we leave him here,' Monroe countered.

He took his leave and paused on the street to look around. There was not much activity in the town, and he wondered if the townsfolk had got wind of the gang's arrival and were taking no chances. Sue emerged from her shop and made her way to the general store. Monroe took out after her, wanting to warn her to remain off the street. As the girl reached the doorway of the store, a man emerged from the building and paused in front of her.

Sue stepped aside, but he moved with her, and she looked up at him enquiringly. When she stepped in the other direction, he did the same, and lifted his hands to grasp her shoulders. Monroe began to run along the street towards them. He had been expecting trouble to blow up from nothing, and it looked as if this was the start of it.

SIX

Monroe reached the front of the store in time to hear Sue remonstrating with the stranger, helpless in the man's grasp. Monroe stepped in close behind her and threw a straight left punch over her shoulder which connected with the centre of the bearded face confronting her. As the man sprawled backwards, Monroe grasped Sue's shoulder and pulled her to one side. She turned a pale face towards him, and relief showed in her blue eyes at the sight of him.

'He's drunk, Wes,' she said fearfully, 'but I don't think he meant any harm.'

'I saw what happened.' He spoke curtly, his gaze on the man. 'Get back out of it, Sue, while I handle this.'

The man had fallen against the wall of the store before sliding down the clapboards to the sidewalk. He was trying unsuccessfully to get to his feet, his bleary eyes fixed on Monroe. When he discovered that he was unable to rise, he reached for his holstered gun. Monroe could have beaten him to the draw, but wanted to avoid gunplay. He stepped forward quickly and kicked the man's wrist as the sixgun slid out of its holster. The pistol went spinning away into the street, and the man flopped backwards and lay gasping.

Monroe grasped the man by his shoulders and pulled him upright, having to support him. At that moment a big man emerged from the store, carrying a sack of provisions. He saw Monroe supporting the stranger, dropped his provisions, and reached for his holstered gun.

'Hold it,' Monroe rapped. 'I'm a deputy sheriff. Stay out of this.'

'He's one of my outfit,' the man replied, staying his hand. 'Circle C. Our herd is outside the town. What's he done?'

Monroe explained and the cattleman shook his head, anger filling his cold blue eyes. He sighed heavily.

'I'm Ed Hardwick, trail boss for Circle C. If no harm is done, I'll take him back to the herd. We don't want any trouble around here.'

'He pulled his gun on me,' Monroe said patiently. 'That's against the law in this county. It's also a by-law for drovers to check in their guns when they come into town. We had some pretty bad trouble from drovers before that law was passed. I can't ignore what happened. If I let this pass, it'll open the door to other offences.'

'No one told us about checking guns when we rode in.' Hardwick was tall, heavy, with a trap-like mouth and hard blue eyes. 'We just dropped in to give the boys a spell from the trail. We ain't finished driving yet, and I'm gonna need every last one of my crew before we get to where we're going. If you jug him and take him before a judge, he'll draw a fine, so state your figure and I'll pay it now. It'll save you going through the rigmarole of the law.'

'Forget the fine,' Monroe decided. 'Just get him out of here. And you better check on the rest of your men. If they're armed, they'll get into trouble. Pull them out of town now, before they're tempted.'

'I'll do that, and thanks.' Hardwick looked at Sue and touched the brim of his Stetson. 'I'm real sorry Pooley made a fool of himself, Miss. He sure overstepped the mark, and then some.'

Hardwick picked up his supplies and then grasped Pooley by the arm. They started along the sidewalk together, the trail boss supporting the drover. Monroe heaved a long sigh, which he stifled when Joseph Falz, the storekeeper, emerged from the store.

'I heard that business,' Falz said sharply. 'What are you trying to do, Wes? We don't get many opportunities to make an extra buck, and with these drovers in town we've struck it rich, but you're running them out before they're ready to go.'

'I'm only concerned with law and order,' Monroe replied. 'We're short-handed as it is because the Town Council won't stump up for more deputies, and no matter what you think, I can't allow drunken drovers to run riot through the town. You wouldn't like it if your wife was accosted in the street. You know of the bad trouble we've had in the past with drovers and herds coming through, and the Town Council decided to put a stop to that. We can't relax the laws now, or we'll be back where we started.'

'I don't like you running the drovers out,' Falz snapped. 'I'm gonna talk with Bentford.'

Monroe stifled an angry reply and turned away. 'I sure wish this day was over,' he told Sue. 'You're gonna have to keep off the street for a spell. That gang of robbers is back, and I haven't located them yet. I'll see you back to your shop. Tell me what time you expect to go home later, and I'll come and escort you.'

Sue was shaken by her encounter with the drover and made no complaint. Monroe took her arm and walked her back along the sidewalk. As they reached the door of her shop he heard the sound of breaking glass along the street and turned quickly to see a drover using a chair to break a front window of the saloon.

'I'm worried about you, Wes,' Sue said. 'All this trouble. What's going on?'

'I don't know, but I'll get to the bottom of it. I have to go. Stay inside until I come back, huh?'

He turned and left her, heading for the saloon. Two more drovers were emerging from the batwings, and they paused to watch their companion wielding the chair. Hardwick was near the saloon now, and the trail boss dropped his supplies and let go of Pooley, who sprawled on the ground. As Monroe hurried towards the saloon, Hardwick grasped the drover causing the disturbance and struck him with a shrewd punch which dropped him on the boardwalk. The two watching drovers complained vigorously.

'Leave him be, Ed,' one of them called. 'The 'tender tried to short-change him. They're a cheating bunch around here.'

'Get the men together and head back to camp,' Hardwick directed. 'I told you no trouble, and if you can't behave then we'll go back to work.'

'Aw, hell,' said the other drover. 'Lay off, can't you? The boys are only letting off a little steam.'

'Take these two along to the stable and put 'em on

their broncs,' Hardwick insisted. 'I'll roust out the rest of them. We're riding back to camp. I warned you what would happen if you stepped out of line. Now get moving.'

Hardwick pushed through the batwings and disappeared inside the saloon. Monroe stayed outside. The two drovers gazed at him impassively, then moved to obey Hardwick's orders. They took hold of their two prostrate pards and hauled them to their feet. As they started along the sidewalk towards the livery barn, the batwings opened and other drovers appeared, protesting vociferously as Hardwick emerged behind them.

'I'll pay for the damage,' the trail boss assured Monroe. 'I'll come in this evening and sort it out.'

'I saw ten of you ride in,' Monroe told him. 'Looks like you've got them all headed out.'

'There are three more out at the camp who are waiting their turn to come in,' Hardwick said. 'I'll keep them out.'

'If they leave their guns behind and behave themselves, there's no reason why they shouldn't come in.'

Hardwick nodded. 'I'll think about it. See you around.'

Monroe walked along the sidewalk towards the livery barn, taking his time, and arrived there as the first of the drovers emerged with his horse. Monroe stood at the end of the sidewalk and waited. Presently all the drovers appeared and set off out of town. Hardwick was the last to leave, and touched the brim of his hat with a forefinger as he rode out.

A sigh gusted through Monroe as he watched the drovers depart. Their leaving made his job much simpler. Now all he had to do was locate the outlaws. He turned and surveyed the street. The town looked peaceful. He saw Joseph Falz emerge from his store, now minus his apron, and stalk along the sidewalk. When the storekeeper had entered the bank, Monroe started back into town.

He paused at the batwings of the saloon and peered into the building. The big room was almost deserted now, and Monroe entered and crossed to the long bar. Pete Feeney, the bartender, was wiping down. Big and heavily built, Feeney was Irish, his fleshy face lumpy with the unmistakable marks of many fists. His brown eyes peered at Monroe from under frowning brows.

'Was it you chased out them drovers?' Feeney demanded. 'Sure, they was only a little bit rowdy. They was just getting warmed up, and their money was rolling over the bar.'

'They were getting out of hand,' Monroe replied. 'You've lost a big window. The next thing, they would have pulled their guns and shot up the town. Why didn't you tell them they were supposed to check their guns before drinking?'

'You're paid to take the risks around here, not me. I'd rather put a stick in a hornets' nest than tell the likes of them what they can or cannot do. My job is to take their money, not stir them up. And can you tell me when Jeff will be getting out of your jail?'

'Have you seen any strangers in town during the past hour?' Monroe countered.

'Sure. Ten of them. They all came from the herd outside town, and they was intent on spending a lot of money until you stopped them. Jeff ain't goin' to be very pleased when he hears about this. He was counting on those drovers to swell the takings, so he was.'

'Have you seen any strangers apart from the drovers?'

'Not even the shadow of one. Do you want to buy a drink, or can I get on with my work?'

Monroe departed. He stood in the batwings and gazed around the street. Glass crunched under his boots when he stepped outside, and he turned and peered in at Feeney.

'You better clean up out here first,' he called. 'This broken glass is dangerous, and it's all over the sidewalk.'

'Sure, and it so happens I've got only one pair of hands, it is. You should have made the man who broke the window clear it up before you sent him packing. I'll get round to it in good time, so I will.'

Monroe went along the sidewalk. He reached the door of the bank as Joseph Falz emerged.

'You weren't satisfied with chasing those drovers out of my store, you had to run them out of town,' Falz complained. 'Is that what you call looking after our interests? You've cost the town a lot of money, Wes. It was a bad thing you did.'

'Can't you think of anything but your profit?'

Monroe walked on in disgust. Falz followed him along the sidewalk, muttering all the time, and Monroe stepped into an alley and paused to let the storekeeper pass. As he did so, a gun blasted from somewhere across the street and a bullet clipped the corner of the building on the left side of the alley. Monroe drew his gun and reached out with his left hand to grasp and drag Falz into cover. Falz fell to the ground, and Monroe was shocked to see blood soaking the storekeeper's chest.

Gunsmoke was drifting from an alley opposite.

Monroe glanced around, then started running across the street, gun cocked and lifted, ready for action. He saw no movement in the alley mouth and paused on the sidewalk in time to catch a glimpse of a figure turning left out of the far end of the alley. He almost fired a shot, but the ambusher was gone before he could react, leaving him with a split-second impression of the man's appearance. A smell of gunsmoke was hanging in the air.

He ran along the sidewalk to the left, instead of chasing along the alley, and stood to one side of the entrance to the next alley, watching for the man. A figure moved into the far end of the alley and paused to look over the back lots. Monroe could see that he was a stranger, and recognized him by his clothes as the ambusher. The man was holding a drawn pistol, and after a couple of moments he left the alley and went on to the left. Monroe repeated his procedure, going left along the sidewalk to flatten himself against the corner of the next alley. A moment later the man came into the alley, and this time he was walking quickly, coming towards the street and Monroe. His gun was back in its holster.

Monroe waited until the man had almost reached him before stepping into the alley mouth, his gun levelled. The man halted, his right hand instinctively moving towards his holster, but he restrained the movement and lifted his hands. He was a stranger, and Monroe was elated. This had to be one of the robbers.

'What's this, a hold up?' the man demanded.

'Get your hands up,' Monroe ordered. 'Why did you shoot at me?'

'I heard a couple of shots.' The man shook his head.

'You got the wrong man. It wasn't me. I've just come out of the stable. I'm gonna take a room at the hotel for the night, and I'll be on my way tomorrow.'

'I said, get your hands up. Come out of the alley and turn your back to me.'

The man obeyed, still protesting, and Monroe drew the pistol nestling in the man's holster. He sniffed the muzzle.

'This has been fired recently,' he observed. 'Two shots were fired, and your gun has two empty cartridges in it. Start walking the way you're facing. The jail is along there. You got some explaining to do, and you can tell me your name to start with.'

'What the hell is this? I'm Bill Oakley. I ain't been in town more than ten minutes. I heard the shots, but I never left the back lots. You got a strange way of dealing the law in this town.'

'Sure. On your way. We'll finish this in the jail. Get moving.'

Oakley opened his mouth to protest; Monroe silenced him with a wave of his pistol. He saw the frustration of a cornered animal in Oakley's eyes as the man turned to walk along the sidewalk. Monroe dropped back a couple of paces and threw a quick glance over his shoulder. He saw several townsmen gathering around the prostrate figure of Joseph Falz, and spotted Doc Twitchell approaching from across the street. Monroe followed the gunman along the board-walk to the jail, and was passed by several townsmen all running towards the spot where Falz was lying.

Sam Aitken was standing in the doorway of the law office. The sheriff was holding his pistol.

'Is Falz dead?' he asked.

'I don't know. I didn't stop to find out. I wanted to get this guy behind bars.'

Aitken stepped back into the office and remained in the background. Monroe pushed Oakley through the doorway and made the man turn out his pockets on to the desk. He pointed to a chair, and Oakley dropped into it, shaking his head. He was tall and broad-shouldered, face unshaven, his range clothes travel-stained. He had the wolfish look of a long rider about him. The contents of his pockets revealed nothing. Monroe stood over him.

'Now, let's have the truth, shall we? Cut out the lies. I saw you running out of the alley when I reached it. I noted your clothes, and when I caught you I got the smell of gunsmoke from your gun. You just missed me with your first shot, and hit Joseph Falz with the second. Two shots have been fired from your gun. So, tell me about it.'

'You're wrong.' Oakley shook his head. 'A man ran out of that alley just before I reached it and took off across the back lots. I just happened to be going in the same direction and you figured I did the shooting.'

'Throw him in a cell and I'll question him, Wes,' Aitken cut in. 'You better get back on the street and check out Falz. We need to know if there's a murder charge to be considered.'

Monroe nodded and picked up the cell keys. He locked Oakley in a cell, then handed the keys to Aitken and departed.

There was a sizeable crowd around Falz when Monroe reached the alley where the shooting had occurred. Doc Twitchell was down on his knees beside the stricken man, working to stem the blood flowing from a wound in Falz's chest. The storekeeper was unconscious, his face ashen. Monroe moved the crowd back, ignoring the spate of questions flung at him. He dropped to one knee beside Twitchell.

'How is he, Doc?'

'It will be touch and go.' Twitchell got to his feet and called for volunteers to help carry the storekeeper to his office. 'You'd better tell Mrs Falz what has happened, Wes.'

Monroe nodded. Four men picked up Falz and began to move along the sidewalk towards the doctor's house. Monroe grasped Twitchell's arm.

'How's that robber making out, Doc?' he asked. 'Bud Hanna.'

'He's pretty bad. I still don't know if he'll make it'

'He's got to be carried over to the jail after dark.'

Twitchell shook his head. 'It's out of the question. Any move would surely kill him.'

Monroe remained standing on the sidewalk while the crowd followed the doctor and his patient. His thoughts were teeming. He needed to locate Mack Hanna and the rest of the gang. They had to be hiding in town. He looked around the street. Evening was drawing on, and shadows were creeping into the corners. He walked to the general store and looked in to find Mrs Falz hurrying towards him. She had obviously received news of the shooting. Her face was expressing shock. She pushed Monroe out of the doorway, closed the door and locked it, then hurried away to the doctor's house.

Monroe walked to the edge of town and looked around in the failing light for the tracks he had followed from Aspen Valley. He recalled that the ten riders had split into two groups and headed for the back lots on either side of the town. Where were they now? They could not have vanished into thin air.

He saw five sets of tracks that had gone to the left, and followed them on foot to the back lots. The ground was still wet from all the rain that had fallen during the past week and the tracks were well defined. They angled away from the row of buildings fronting the street and he looked ahead to judge their general direction. He thought they had entered the town, but saw that he had been wrong. The tracks bypassed Bitter Creek, heading south. He hurried back to where the tracks had split into two groups, and followed those passing the town on the right. When they reached the southern end of the street they kept going, but a few yards on two sets of tracks turned and headed into the town. Monroe halted, and gazed after the other three. They were heading south.

He shook his head, trying to work out what was in Mack Hanna's mind. Hanna would think his father, if still alive, was in the jail, but it would be a simple matter for the gang boss to find out what had happened after the failed bank raid. When he learned that his father was being treated in Doc Twitchell's house, he could easily hold the doctor and Mrs Twitchell hostage until his father could be moved.

Monroe wanted Bud Hanna behind bars. As far as he could see, it was the only way to control the situation. With enough armed men inside the jail, there would be little chance of a jail-break. He started walking into the main street, almost invisible now in the growing darkness. His thoughts were teeming. The two sets of tracks entering the town pointed to Bill Oakley and Jake Wells being members of the Hanna gang. They had apparently been sent in to check on the situation in Bitter Creek, but Wells had ambushed Monroe in the stable and Oakley tried to shoot him down from the alley.

Acting on a hunch, Monroe turned aside and went into the stable. There was a single lantern hanging from a nail to the right of the big open doorway, which did not provide much light for those who had business inside. Monroe moved through the shadows, guided by another lantern inside the office. Fred Barlow, the ostler, was seated at the desk in the office, thumbing casually through a magazine. He got to his feet when he saw Monroe, his face alive with curiosity.

'What was that shooting earlier?' Barlow demanded. 'All the drovers left half an hour ago.'

'Are there any other strangers in town, Fred? Has anyone ridden in during the last hour?'

'Only one, far as I know. He turned up about half an hour before the shooting. Left his horse in a stall and paid for a couple of days' feed.'

Monroe named and described Oakley. Barlow nodded.

'That's him. Got the look of a long rider about him.'

'That's what I thought. He fired a couple of shots from an alley, missed me, and hit Joseph Falz, who was in my company.'

'Is Falz dead?'

'Doc thinks he'll make it. I'm thinking Oakley is a member of the Hanna gang, although I can't think why he would want to shoot me. I've never seen him before, and I don't think he was in Bitter Creek before today.'

'He ain't one of those drovers, huh?'

'I'll check him out with the trail boss. Show me Oakley's horse.'

Barlow showed Monroe the stall where Oakley's horse was standing. Monroe saw the saddle and saddle-bags nearby, and checked the contents of the bags, finding nothing of interest. He took his leave and went back to the law office, wondering where Jake Wells had left his horse.

Sam Aitken was sitting at his desk, head in his hands, his elbows propped on top of the desk.

'Are you all right, Sam?' Monroe enquired. 'You're looking like all hell. I reckon you're doing too much on your first day back.'

Aitken heaved a long sigh and straightened in his seat, shaking his head. His face was pale and he was sweating.

'I ain't feeling right, not by a long rope,' he said. 'I didn't get anything more out of Oakley or Wells. When I questioned them, I got the feeling they knew each other, although both denied it. How are things around town?'

'Quiet now. Doc thinks Falz should pull through. He told me Bud Hanna is too ill to be moved, but I won't be happy if we can't get him in a cell after dark.'

'I know what you mean, but we better not move him if Twitchell is against it. Bud Hanna alive and at the Doc's place is better than him being dead in a cell.'

'Leaving him with Doc is like giving Mack Hanna a lever to use against us.' Monroe sat down on a corner of the desk and thumbed back the brim of his Stetson. 'Why don't you go home and get some rest, Sam? I can handle things around here. Where's Joe, by the way?'

'I gave him some time off. He's been pushing it

pretty hard while I've been sick. He's not getting any younger, and he's been having a go at me to make him a deputy. When I told him he's too old to tote a badge, he went off in a huff.'

'I agree with you. Becoming a deputy is the only thing Joe has been talking about for weeks. I think you're right. Joe is OK as a jailer, but I reckon being a deputy is beyond him.'

'I reckon we'll have to find a new jailer now. I don't think Joe will carry on.'

'I'll find him and have a word.' Monroe stifled a sigh. 'We're short-handed as it is. Joe is better than nothing as the jailer. Hold on here until I get back, then you'd better go home. You ain't looking at all well, Sam.'

He left the office. Full darkness had settled over the town and a keen breeze was blowing along the wide street. Lights glowed in many windows along the length of the street, and Monroe thought of Sue, waiting in her shop for him to return to her. He set off to see her, intending to look up Joe Parfitt later, thinking that the jailer would be in the saloon trying to drink away his disappoinment at failing to get a deputy badge. Parfitt had set great store on making it to deputy sheriff.

The general store was in darkness, and Monroe paused outside, wondering about Joseph Falz. Mrs Falz would probably stay overnight at the Doc's place, which meant the store would be deserted and needed extra attention. He was about to move on to the dress shop when a crash inside the deserted store alerted him. It sounded as if someone had blundered into something in the darkness and knocked it over.

Monroe drew his gun, his suspicions aroused. The press of trouble that had descended upon him with the advent of the Hanna gang had driven all thoughts of the local thief out of his mind, and he wondered if the unknown law-breaker was taking advantage of the situation.

SEVEN

Monroe entered the alley and went along to the store's side door. He tried it gently, found it was locked, and peered in through a window. The interior was too dark for him to make out details. He stood listening intently, thinking of the unknown thief who, by his exploits, was making life difficult for him. He moved to the rear of the store and found a small window of four panes of glass standing open, and one of the panes was broken. The thief had evidently reached in through the broken pane and unbolted the window.

Certain that the thief was still inside, Monroe eased back into the shadows and waited with a patience that grew with the job of lawman. He strained his ears to pick up unnatural sounds inside the store, and heard someone again stumbling over something in the darkness inside the building. He crouched and waited, with ready gun.

Minutes later, a bulky object was thrown from the open window, and then a figure climbed over the sill and dropped to the ground. Monroe reached forward with his gun and jabbed the muzzle into the man's side.

'Hands up!' he rapped. 'I got you to rights. Get 'em high.'

There was a gasp of shock from the thief and his hands shot up above his shoulders.

'Is that you, Wes?' a voice demanded.

'Sure is, and I've been trying to catch you for weeks. I can't see a thing. Who are you?'

'It's me, Joe Parfitt. You got me hook, line and sinker. I ain't armed, Wes.'

'*Joe?* Are you the thief I've been after all this time?'

'Would it be any use denying it?'

'But why, Joe? You don't need to rob.'

'I was sick of being turned down for a badge. I reckoned if I caused some trouble around town, the Council would decide you needed an extra deputy and give me a chance.'

'Robbing folks ain't the way to work your way into law-dealing. What have you stolen?'

'Just some supplies. All the takings are in there. I wouldn't touch money. I never took much of anything.'

'What the hell am I gonna do about you?' Monroe demanded. 'Heck, I don't even have to think about it. I got to run you in, Joe. Pick up that sack and we'll talk to the sheriff about this.'

Parfitt picked up the large sack and they continued along the back lots to the law office. Monroe's thoughts were in turmoil. They needed Parfitt as a jailer, especially now, with prisoners to be guarded and a gang of robbers on the loose. Parfitt entered the office and Wes followed him. Aitken was seated at the desk. The sheriff was looking worse than before, and Monroe felt a pang of concern stab through him.

'I got to go home, Wes,' Aitken said. 'I reckon I've

done too much for my first day back on duty. It's good of you to come in after I gave you the night off, Joe.'

Monroe went to the sheriff's side. Aitken got to his feet and staggered as he came around the desk. He would have fallen if Monroe hadn't reached out to support him.

'Stay here, Joe, until I get back,' Monroe ordered. 'We've got another new prisoner in the cells. He tried to kill me, so be careful around him. We'll talk after I've got Sam home.'

'Sure thing, Wes.' Parfitt nodded. 'You know you can rely on me to do my job.'

Parfitt went behind the desk and sat down. He opened the sack he had brought from the store and rummaged inside it as Monroe led the sheriff out of the office. Monroe felt frustration boiling up inside him as they made their way to the sheriff's home.

Mack Hanna was frustrated also. He had dropped Oakley and Wells off outside Bitter Creek with instructions to go into town and get information about Bud Hanna's condition, and to kill Monroe. The deputy was too dangerous to be left alive. Hanna dared not show his face in Bitter Creek because he knew he could be recognized, and he was angry because he could not trust anyone to do exactly what he wanted – to get his father out of the clutches of the law and take the money that was in the bank.

Night was falling when they reached Denton's place. As outlaws, they were accustomed to living rough, and put their horses under cover where they could graze. They made camp behind the shack, which afforded some shelter from the ceaseless wind, and Hanna's bad humour faded after they had eaten, but his patience suffered badly as time passed and neither Oakley nor Wells showed up. He sensed that something had gone wrong. He needed to know his father's fate and, despite the promptings of common sense, which advised him to remain where he was, he saddled up, warned his men to stay put until he returned, and rode to Bitter Creek.

Jack Thompson had talked at length about the town during their long evenings around a camp-fire, and Hanna knew the place as if he had lived there for years. Thompson had drawn maps in the dust, highlighting the bank, the law office and other places that would interest men determined to rob the community. They all learned that Jeff Teague was a rogue who would do anything to make a fast buck, and they had listened to Thompson's hopes for the future, which he intended to be spent with Sue Walton.

The lights of the town shimmered through the darkness when Hanna rode in close to Luke Baine's place of business on the back lots. He tethered his horse in the shadows behind the house, peered through a lighted window, and saw Baine and his wife eating a meal. He made for the street, wondering what had become of Oakley and Wells. Their business should have been completed in a matter of minutes. He assumed that they had taken time out to visit the saloon, and decided to teach them a lesson when he caught up with them.

He went to the saloon and peered into the big room through one of the front windows. Teague he knew by description, but the saloonman was not in evidence. Hanna passed along the alley beside the saloon and tried the door that gave access to Teague's private quarters. The door was locked, but Hanna threw his shoulder against it a couple of times and it flew open. He entered and closed the door, holding it in place with the back of a chair under the door handle.

A search of the private quarters showed the place was deserted, and Hanna wondered where Teague might be. He opened the door leading into the bar and Feeney, the bartender, caught the movement of the door and left the bar. He approached Hanna, who remained where he was, his hand close to the butt of his gun.

'How did you get in there?' Feeney demanded.

'Through the side door. I need to see Teague.'

Feeney nodded. He was accustomed to strangers dropping in on Jeff Teague.

'It's visiting the jail you'll be, if you want to see Teague,' he said. 'Sure, they've jailed him for no reason at all. A law-abiding citizen going about his honest work is Jeff Teague, and they threw him in the jail.'

'What for?' Hanna wanted to know.

'That's what everyone is asking.' Feeney shook his head. 'There's no rhyme or reason why. Jack Thompson came back two days ago, and the minute he showed his face he caused trouble. Some men have the knack of doing that. He's in the jail, too.'

'What's Thompson in for?'

'They're saying he paid an outlaw to shoot the sheriff. There was an attempted robbery at the bank yesterday, so there was. Since then the town has been in uproar, it has, and there are Texas cattle-drovers with a herd just outside town. The law department is running around like a chicken with its head cut off. Two strangers came in earlier, and both are in jail. One tried to stab Monroe, the deputy, and the other took a

107

couple of shots at him. Both failed because Monroe can fight his weight in wildcats, that he can. You're a stranger. What's your business with Teague? Mebbe I can help you. Teague wouldn't want me to turn away any man who comes round asking for him.'

'What happened to the bank robber who was shot in the street?'

'You'll be meaning Bud Hanna, the father of Mack Hanna, no less. They say he's likely to die, but is still holding on. He's lying in the doctor's house, that he is, and they say Luke Baine, the undertaker, has already measured him for his box.'

'Where's the doctor's place?'

'Turn right on the street. Doctor Twitchell's house is on the left, past Meeke's gun shop. You can't miss it, if you keep your eyes open. The doctor's shingle is beside the door.'

'Thanks. I'll leave by the side door.' Hanna turned away. 'You better get this door fixed,' he observed as he departed. 'Someone's kicked it in.'

He went along the alley to the street, and spent some minutes peering around from the shadows. A slow fire was burning inside him. Oakley and Wells had fouled up, Thompson was in jail, and Bud was on the danger list. He walked along the street, keeping to the shadows, and paused at the house with the nameplate outside. He knocked at the door, which was opened by Mrs Twitchell.

'Evening, ma'am.' Hanna forced a note of unaccustomed affability into his voice. 'I heard you got a wounded bank robber here. I'm Frank Howard, State Deputy Marshal. Can you tell me how that robber is doing? I've come from Helena to take him back there.'

'You'd better talk to my husband, the doctor. He'll be able to give you a report.'

'No need to worry your husband, ma'am. I'll be in town several days. Will the prisoner be ready to travel by the end of the week, do you think?'

'I don't think so. He's been very badly wounded. Are you sure you won't come in and talk to my husband?'

'Not now, ma'am. I got to check with the sheriff. I'll drop by later.'

Hanna turned away, his mind racing with conjecture. Bud was still alive. He went on along the street and slipped into the alley opposite the law office, where he paused to study his surroundings for some minutes before crossing the street and peering into the office through the big front window. He saw Joe Parfitt seated at the desk and wondered where Monroe, the deputy, had gone. He was tempted to enter the office and demand the release of his men, and stood hesitating while he considered the action, sniffing the air like a lobo wolf as he tried to decide.

Before he was aware of his actions, Hanna had pushed open the door of the office and entered, drawing his gun as he did so. Parfitt looked up, and froze at the sight of the levelled gun.

'Get your keys,' Hanna rapped. 'Make it quick. I want my men out of here fast.'

'You're Mack Hanna!' Parfitt sprang up. He snatched the key-ring from its hook, dropped it in his haste, and bent to scoop it up. 'Anything you say, Mr Hanna. I ain't wearing a gun and I won't give you any trouble. The cells are right this way.' He hurried towards the door leading into the cell block.

Hanna followed closely. Parfitt unlocked the doors

of the occupied cells. Jack Thompson was the last to be released, and he grabbed Parfitt and shook him violently.

'Get out of here,' snarled Hanna at his men. 'I want to talk to him, so leave him be, Jack. We're wasting time. Jack, you stay here. The rest of you get the weapons in the office. Watch the street, huh?' He menaced Parfitt with his gun. 'Where's the deputy?'

Parfitt cringed. His face was pale, taut with fear.

'He took the sheriff home some time ago. Sam Aitken ain't been well. I don't know where Monroe could be now. He's out there somewhere, probably looking for you.'

Hanna struck Parfitt across the head with the barrel of his pistol, tumbling him to the floor. He looked at Thompson, his eyes smouldering with a blend of rage and hatred. It was all he could do to stop short of shooting Thompson.

'You ain't done well, Jack,' he ground out. 'I got it figured you were more interested in getting the sheriff's badge than pushing our interests. You were supposed to kill the sheriff, but it ain't happened. When we came into town to hit the bank, the law was in the bank waiting for us to enter. That means someone talked, either you or Sullivan. The deputy, Monroe, shot Sullivan and jugged him, and if I hadn't sent a couple of the boys along unknown to you to watch over things, Sullivan would still be in jail. Then you set Ike and Jake the job of killing that deputy when I wouldn't have sent either of them to the store to get a stick of candy. So I lost two more men, and Monroe is still running around loose. On top of that, Wells and Oakley came in to finish the deputy and they wound up in here.'

'It was just bad luck, Mack.' Thompson shrugged. 'Everything seemed to go wrong, but I can put it right by killing Monrroe.'

'Monroe ain't the big problem right now. Bud is bad hurt at the doc's. We got to get him out of there. Take two of the men, get a wagon, and haul Bud out to the Denton place. Grab the doc's wife while you're at it, and we'll take her along as a hostage.'

'That don't sound like a good idea, Mack. Snatch a woman and you'll rouse up the whole town.'

'Who's asking you? Just do like I say. We need a hostage. Once we get Bud clear we'll come back and empty the bank. Now get moving.'

'Anything you say, Mack. You're the boss.'

'Damn right I am. So hop to it. We'll figure out our next move later. This time you better do everything right, Jack. One more bad play and it'll be all over for you. Take Wells and Oakley with you.'

Thompson turned and hurried out. Hanna kicked the unconscious Parfitt in the ribs and went into the law office. The gun rack had been forced open and weapons taken. Cartridges had been found. The outlaws were watching the street. Teague stood motionless by the door, his expression showing unease. Hanna regarded the saloonman with narrowed eyes, wondering if he could use him.

'You're Teague, huh?' he asked. 'What are you going to do? You can't stick around town, or they'll arrest you again. Do you wanta ride with us?'

'I ain't cut out for that life.' Teague shook his head emphatically 'Maybe you better lock me in a cell and I'll try to bluff my way out of this. I can't run. Everything I have is tied up in the saloon.'

'You said it.' Hanna nodded. 'Get back in a cell and I'll turn the key. That's all I can do for you. I'll kill Monroe when I see him, and that might help you out. OK?'

'Sure. Thanks.'

Teague wiped sweat from his face and went back into the cell block. Hanna followed, and locked Teague in a cell. He dragged the inert Parfitt into another cell and slammed the door.

'See you around,' he told the disconsolate saloon-man, and departed to look around the town.

He was standing in the shadows opposite the doctor's house when Thompson arrived with a wagon. Thompson and Wiley went into the house, while Oakley remained with the vehicle. Time flitted by and Hanna's impatience grew. He was about to go over to the wagon, when the door of the house was opened and Thompson emerged, holding the front end of a stretcher. Doc Twitchell was holding the rear end and between them they hoisted the stretcher into the wagon. Wiley was standing with Mrs Twitchell, a gun in his hand.

The doctor stepped back beside his wife and placed a hand protectively on her shoulder.

'I told you, she's going along with us to take care of the patient,' Thompson said in a loud voice. 'She'll come back to you when we pull out.'

'I'll go with you instead,' Twitchell said. 'I told you the man can't be moved yet. I'll have to come along, because he'll surely die if he doesn't get good treatment.'

'I got my orders.' Thompson reached out and grasped Mrs Twitchell's arm.

Twitchell struck at Thompson, and Wiley swung his pistol, crashing the barrel against the side of the doctor's head. Twitchell fell to the ground. Mrs Twitchell bent over him, her voice echoing across the street as she protested. Hanna started out of the shadows, angry at the disturbance. All it needed now was for Monroe to appear.

Thompson grasped Mrs. Twitchell and swung her into the back of the wagon then sprang in beside her. Wiley joined him and Oakley whipped up the team. Hanna heaved a sigh of relief as the vehicle moved along the street at a fast clip. He remained watching until it disappeared from sight and the noise of its passing faded away.

Twitchell suddenly got up from the street and staggered into his house. Hanna heard him calling for his wife. When there was no reply, Twitchell reappeared and hurried along the street towards the law office. Hanna grinned and went in the opposite direction. He collected his horse from behind Luke Baine's house and set out for the Denton place, staying back from the wagon to guard against pursuit.

Doc Twitchell staggered into the law office, breathing heavily. He stared around, unable to believe the place was deserted. The door to the cells was ajar and he went to it, jerking it wide.

'Wes? Joe? Are you around?' he called.

'I'm locked in a cell,' Joe Parfitt replied.

Twitchell held a hand to his head as he entered the cell block. He saw Teague sitting on the bunk in the nearest cell. The jailer was next to the saloonman.

'There's been hell to pay,' Parfitt groaned. 'Mack Hanna was here and turned the prisoners loose.

113

They're going to your place to grab that wounded outlaw.'

'They did that right enough,' Twitchell replied. 'Where is Wes?'

'He took Sam home. I ain't seen him since.' Parfitt touched his head and then looked at the blood on his fingers. 'The keys are on the floor over there, Doc. Turn me loose and I'll raise the alarm.'

'They took my wife with them.' Twitchell found the keys and opened the cell door. 'I'm afraid for her life, Joe.'

Parfitt sighed heavily. 'We need to find Wes. He'll know what to do.'

Monroe had taken the sheriff home, and Aitken collapsed without warning just before they reached his house. Monroe bent over the ailing lawman, shaking his head. Aitken was unconscious. Wes picked him up and carried him the last few yards to the house. He kicked the door and Martha opened it quickly. She uttered a gasp of shock as Monroe carried her husband in.

'This way.' She led him up the stairs to the bedroom.

Aitken came back to his senses as Monroe put him on the bed.

'I'm sorry to be a trouble,' he muttered.

'You should have stayed away from the office,' Monroe told him. 'To hell with the Town Council. You stay here until you're better. I'll fetch Twitchell to you, Sam.'

'No.' Aitken clutched at Monroe's arm. 'I'll be OK. I'm exhausted, that's all. I'll be right as rain in the morning. Just let me sleep.'

Monroe looked at Martha and she nodded.

'Do as he says, Wes. Come and see him tomorrow. I won't let him come to work until I'm certain he's well, even if I have to take a gun to him.'

Monroe shook his head and departed. He was worried about the situation. He walked to the main street and saw four men on the sidewalk in front of the saloon. Unable to recognize them, he went forward, then recognized one of them as Ed Hardwick, the trail boss. As he drew within earshot, he heard Hardwick laying down the law to the three drovers, whose hard faces were highlighted by the front window of the saloon.

'You sure you ain't got weapons on you?' Hardwick was saying. 'I don't want any trouble at all, you got that? There was trouble this afternoon, and I won't stand for any more. I got to pay damages now, so spare me. Have a drink and then come back to the herd.'

The three drovers nodded and trooped into the saloon. Hardwick heard Monroe's boots on the sidewalk and turned to face him.

'Howdy,' he greeted. 'You won't have any trouble this evening. There's only three of my crew in. I've barred the rest. If they can't act right, then they'll stay clear of town. I was coming to see you. Tell me what the damage is from this afternoon and I'll pay you.'

'Talk to the 'tender inside,' Monroe told him. 'There's just the window to pay for.'

'We'll be moving on in the morning,' Hardwick said. 'See you around, huh?'

Monroe nodded and Hardwick went into the saloon. Monroe turned and went back along the street to the dress shop, where a light in the window indicated that Sue was still working. He tapped at the door and she came in answer.

115

'Wes, it's good to see you,' she said, and Monroe's cares seemed to dissipate at the warmth in her voice. 'Would you like a coffee?'

'I would.' He suppressed a sigh as he entered the shop and closed the door. 'The town seems to be quiet at the moment. I reckon I can take a break before doing the rounds.'

He explained about the sheriff, and Sue tut-tutted.

'You shouldn't be on your own with all this trouble around you.' She busied herself with making coffee. 'What are you going to do if that gang comes back? You can't fight them on your own. When are you going to get more help, Wes? You can't go on like this.'

'I'll talk to Luke Baine tomorrow. I need a couple of deputies to back me. There's a big danger to the town while that wounded outlaw is in the doc's house.'

He thought of the ten sets of tracks he had followed heading into Bitter Creek, and had to fight against the urge to get up and start looking more intently for the gang. He fancied that Abe Bentford would back him with additional help after the abortive bank raid, and was determined to pursue the matter.

Sue set a cup of coffee before him. Her lovely face was clouded with worry, and her blue eyes showed concern as she sat down opposite him.

'How's your work going, Sue?'

'It will be done on time.'

'I caught the thief who's been making trouble.'

'Who is it?'

Monroe shook his head. 'I can't say at the moment. It's just another problem to be faced.'

'I'm curious. It's got to be a local man. He even tried to break in here a few weeks ago. I still wonder what he was after. Surely he wasn't going to steal a dress!'

Monroe did not smile. 'I wouldn't be surprised at anything he took. Most of what he has lifted wasn't worth the taking.'

'So why is he stealing? Does he *want* to be caught and jailed?'

'I'll ask him when I see him again.'

Monroe found himself relaxing in Sue's company, and stiffened himself against it. He had work to do. He drained his cup.

'That was good. I'll have to come and see you more often.'

'Would you like another cup?'

'I would, but I daren't.' He smiled. 'I've got a lot to do.'

He stood up, and as they walked into the front shop someone hammered on the street door with a heavy fist.

'Wes, are you in there? We've had trouble in the jail.'

'That's Parfitt.' Wes opened the door and the jailer practically fell across the threshold. 'What's wrong, Joe?'

Parfitt blurted out the fact that Mack Hanna had walked into the office with a gun in his hand and freed the prisoners. Monroe grasped Parfitt's arm and hurried him out of the shop. He started at a run towards the law office, dragging Parfitt along with him, but a shot blasted out the deep silence lying over the town and muted echoes sounded.

Monroe stopped as if he had taken a bullet. He turned swiftly, trying to pick up the direction from which the sound of the shot had come.

'The saloon,' gasped Parfitt. 'It came from there.'

117

Monroe ran along the sidewalk, drawing his gun as he did so. Trouble was looming over the town, and this was likely the start of it.

EIGHT

Monroe thrust open the batwings and ran into the saloon, his gun levelled. He halted abruptly when he saw Pete Feeney standing behind the bar with a pistol in his right hand. Two of the three drovers had their hands shoulder-high – the third was lying on the floor. A puff of gunsmoke was drifting across the bar.

'What's going on?' Monroe paced forward, gun at his hip.

'Sure, the feller on the floor pulled a knife on me for no reason at all.' Feeney waggled his pistol. 'Just three of them drovers in here having a quiet drink, and one of them starts something from nothing.'

'Put your gun away, Pete.' Monroe looked at the drovers. 'You got anything to say?'

'I don't know why Charlie pulled the knife,' one of them said. 'He's been moody for weeks. Mebbe he picked up a dose of trail-fever.'

'Charlie heard the 'tender short-changed one of our pards this afternoon,' the other said. 'He was out to even the score.'

Monroe bent over the fallen drover. There was blood on the man's shirt, high on the right shoulder.

'It doesn't look too bad,' he opined. 'You two better pick him up and carry him to the doc's place. Do you want to make a charge against him, Pete?'

Feeney shook his head. 'Let them take him out to their camp when the doc gets through with him.'

Monroe nodded. The two drovers picked up their wounded companion and carried him out. Joe Parfitt was standing by the batwings. He came forward to the bar and asked for a whiskey. Monroe examined the jailer's head.

'You've had a heavy blow behind your ear, Joe, and you look awful. Do you want to go home and rest?'

'No. You've got a lot on your plate. I haven't told you the half of it yet. Doc Twitchell is waiting in the office for you. Mack Hanna took that outlaw out of the doc's house. They fetched a wagon and hauled him out of town, and took Doc's wife with them as a hostage. The doc wants you to ride with him to get Mrs Twitchell back.'

'The hell you say!' Monroe turned and ran out of the saloon. He passed the two drovers on the sidewalk and paused to tell them to take their wounded pard to the jail. He continued to the office and found the doctor pacing up and down. Twitchell's face was grey with shock.

'Did Joe tell you what's happened, Wes?'

'I just heard.'

'They took Mattie. I fear for her life, Wes. They won't get far with Bud Hanna. The move is gonna kill him for sure, and I don't see Mattie walking away from this. Jack Thompson is helping the robbers. He showed up with the wagon. He's a real bad lot, Wes.'

'Which way did they go, Doc?'

120

'South. It's a wonder you didn't see the wagon leaving town. Where were you?'

'I'll ride out and look for the wagon. It won't get far. You'd better stay here, Doc. There's a wounded drover being brought in, with a slug in his shoulder.' Monroe turned to the door as Parfitt came into the office. 'Stay here with the doc, Joe, and do what you can to help.'

'You won't see much out there,' Parfitt said, 'even though there's a moon. You should wait for morning.'

Monroe shook his head and departed. He hurried to the livery barn and entered the stable, gun in hand, expecting trouble, but the place was silent and still. He saddled up quickly, led the horse outside and swung into the saddle. A sense of relief filled him as he hit the trail. It looked like the waiting was over.

The night was overcast, but there were breaks in the dark mantle where stars gleamed remotely. The moon shone fitfully, although it was obscured intermittently by scudding clouds. Faint silvery light illuminated the rough landscape, but the night seemed twice as dark when the moon was covered by cloud. A faint breeze blew into Monroe's face as he rode. He halted every fifty yards or so to listen intently for sounds of the wagon.

He expected the outlaws to leave at least one man in their rear to check for pursuit, and was in no hurry to overhaul his quarry. He did not want a running fight with these desperate men because they had Mattie Twitchell, and he knew they would not hesitate to use the woman to gain any advantage they required.

Presently he heard the grating of wheels on the trail, and moved off to the right to avoid the rear guard. He knew the area intimately and tried to guess the destina-

121

tion of the wagon, although it did not matter where Mack Hanna was headed, because there was no escape for the outlaw.

It soon became apparent that the wagon was making for the old Denton place. Monroe swung out in a wide circle and put a ridge between himself and the sound of the moving vehicle. He rode fast, and soon spotted the derelict shack. His narrowed eyes picked up the faint glimmer of a camp-fire, and he rode into a thicket and tethered his horse to a bush. He moved closer on foot, snaking forward like an Indian, and reached the shadows surrounding the fire as the wagon arrived. He noted several men lounging around the fire.

He lay in cover and watched Jack Thompson jump down from the high seat of the vehicle, and recognized Oakley and Wells. Mattie Twitchell was helped out of the wagon and made to sit by the fire, which was replenished with wood until flickering firelight threw leaping shadows on the taut faces around it. Mack Hanna rode in and dismounted.

'I got a sneaking feeling we were followed,' Hanna said. 'Jack, take Oakley with you and ride back to town. Go for that deputy, and this time make sure he dies. When you've killed him, send Oakley back with the word, and we'll come back to town and put Bud under cover. I reckon we oughta take over the saloon until Bud is fit to travel.'

Thompson looked around. 'Sure, if that's what you want, Mack. I'll have to borrow a horse, and I need a pistol.'

'Take mine.' Mack Hanna handed over the reins. 'Here's my spare gun. Watch for trouble on the way in.'

122

'You don't need Mrs Twitchell out here,' Thompson said.

'Why do you think we brought her? Being the doc's wife, she'll be good at nursing. She can look after Bud. Jake, you stick close to her. If anyone shows up to try and grab her away, you know what to do.'

'Sure.' Jake Wells chuckled hoarsely. 'That won't be a problem.'

'Handle it better than your attempt to kill that deputy,' Hanna responded.

Thompson and Oakley left the camp. Monroe slipped away and went back to his horse. If there had been one chance in ten of rescuing Mrs Twitchell he would have tried it, but the odds were too great. He set off back to town, circling, riding fast, and was waiting at a front corner of the livery barn when Thompson and Oakley arrived. They took their horses into the stable and, when they emerged minutes later, Thompson paused in the wide doorway.

'Bill, I got a job to do before we get down to Hanna's business.'

'Don't do it, Jack. Hanna ain't the man to fool around with. If it's some woman you want to visit, then forget it. I wouldn't put it past Hanna to follow us in and watch us. I reckon the sooner we nail that deputy, and I head back to camp, the better. Wait till Hanna comes into town before you try your own thing.'

'This business won't wait. It *is* a woman I've got to see, but not like you think. I'm planning to head south with her when we've cleaned out the bank. You go along to the law office and check for Monroe. He could be anywhere, but don't take him on yourself. You've tried that once tonight, and proved you ain't in his class. Leave him to me. I want the pleasure of killing him myself. Just find him and watch him. I'll catch up with you later.'

'I don't like it,' Oakley muttered.

'Do like I say.' Thompson crossed the street and disappeared into the darkness.

Oakley stood gazing after Thompson for several moments, then shook his head and drew his pistol. He checked the weapon before sliding it back into his holster. Monroe eased forward around the corner, cocking his gun as he did so. He was barely ten feet from Oakley.

'I'll walk along to the jail with you,' Monroe called.

Oakley spun around, right hand dropping to his gun, but halted the movement when he saw Monroe's levelled gun. His hands shot up shoulder-high.

'You must like the inside of my jail,' Monroe said. 'Hold still and I'll take your gun.'

Oakley obeyed reluctantly. Monroe snaked the gun out of Oakley's holster and stuck it in the waistband of his pants.

'You know where the jail is, so head for it. Any wrong ideas and you're dead.' Monroe jabbed the muzzle of his pistol against Oakley's spine. 'Don't make a sound. I wanta surprise Thompson after I've taken care of you.'

Oakley came swinging around, an outflung elbow catching Monroe's gun-hand and knocking it aside. Monroe was ready for such a move, but was caught by the speed with which it was executed. He ducked his head to the left as Oakley's fist came whirling in for his jaw, and the blow missed by a hair's breadth. Oakley cursed and threw a punch with his left hand, slamming his bunched knuckles into Monroe's stomach.

Monroe eased back, threw his right in a short, power-ful arc, and connected with Oakley's jaw. The man stag-gered back, but steadied himself and lifted a boot. Monroe turned sideways and took the toe of the boot on his thigh. He struck with his pistol, catching Oakley on the left temple and sending him crashing to the sidewalk.

'On your feet.' Monroe waggled his gun. 'You're keen on learning things the hard way, huh?'

Oakley pushed himself to his feet and staggered along the sidewalk without comment. Monroe followed a couple of paces behind, his gun ready. The street was deserted, but there were lights here and there along its length. Monroe saw a light in Sue's shop. He guessed Thompson was paying the girl another visit, and fought down his impatience. Sue would keep Thompson occu-pied until he could be tackled.

They were passing the alley beside the dress shop when a movement in the darkness there attracted Monroe's attention. He turned swiftly, but was too late to avoid the heavy fist that came out of the shadows and crashed against his jaw. The street seemed to tilt and swing as he wilted under the blow. He dropped to his knees, trying desperately to lift his gun into play, but his whirling senses betrayed him and he was unable to resist. A booted foot came up out of the shadows, took him flush on the jaw, and he fell forward and smashed his face against the obdurate sidewalk.

Rough hands seized hold of Monroe's shoulders and he was dragged to his feet. He lifted his right knee instinctively, slamming it into his assailant's groin. He heard a low groan and forced himself to react. His gun was gone from his hand and he ducked to his left, anticipating another punch. His sudden move overbalanced him and he went sideways, but he managed to stay on his feet. He reached out with his right hand, throwing a punch at the dark shape looming up before him.

His knuckles slammed solidly against a jaw. He shook his head to clear his senses and moved forward, hearing Oakley to his left turning to join in the fight. He slid away to the right, moving in a half-circle to place his unknown assailant between Oakley and himself. Oakley threw a punch that missed Monroe and landed on the other man. Monroe heard an oath from the stranger, and recognized Jack Thompson's voice. He kicked at Oakley and the man folded instantly, cursing in agony. He dropped a hand to his holster and found it empty, then remembered that he had dropped the weapon.

Sue opened the door of the shop at that moment and yellow lamplight shafted out across the sidewalk. Monroe saw Oakley on the boards, and Thompson was turning swiftly, boring in to continue the violence. Monroe could make out Thompson's big figure and taut features in the light issuing from the dress shop, and let rip with two quick punches that slammed into Thompson's body. Thompson backed off, reaching for his gun. Monroe lunged forward and hit Thompson, his head down and hands reaching out to grasp and hold. His head caught Thompson in the chest and knocked him back on his heels.

Monroe surged upright, throwing heavy punches, wanting to punish Thompson, but the ex-deputy drew his gun and slammed the barrel against Monroe's skull. Monroe went down and stayed there. Thompson stood over Monroe, gun levelled at the deputy's heart. Sue's voice came to Thompson as if from a great distance, and he shook his head. His senses seemed to slip back into focus.

'Don't kill him, Jack!' Sue reached out and grabbed Thompson's arm. 'I'll go away with you now if you spare him. Shoot him and I'll never speak to you again, and I'll take a gun to you the first chance I get.'

'It's a deal.' Thompson holstered his gun. 'Let's get outta here. I only came back to this burg for you. Let's go.'

Oakley sat up, and Thompson stepped forward a half pace and kicked out with his right foot. His toe took Oakley on the chin and stretched him out again. Thompson grasped Sue's arm and hurried her away along the street, leaving the door of the dress shop wide open.

Monroe regained his senses slowly and looked around, but there was no sign of Thompson and Sue. He saw Oakley stretched out on the boardwalk and pushed himself to his feet, trying to recollect what had happened. He saw his gun lying a few feet away and picked it up. He checked Oakley, found the man unconscious, and went to the door of the dress shop, thinking that Sue had returned there. He called her name, but there was no reply.

He turned his attention to Oakley, who was beginning to stir. Monroe's body ached in a dozen different places.

'On your feet, Oakley,' he commanded. He pulled a pair of handcuffs off the back of his belt and snapped one cuff on Oakley, then passed the second cuff around an awning post and clicked it on the outlaw's other wrist.

'Where's Thompson?' Oakley demanded.

'You tell me.' Monroe went into the shop, gun in hand, and searched it in vain. He fingered the bump on his head where Thompson had hit him, and grimaced. He was taking more than his share of lumps these days.

He went back to Oakley, freed the man from the awning post, and Oakley staggered to his feet and continued towards the jail. Monroe followed him, ready for further resistance, but it seemed that the outlaw had satiated his desire to resist.

They reached the jail without further incident, and Oakley thrust open the door. Joe Parfitt stood up at the desk, a shotgun in his hands. Doc Twitchell appeared in the doorway of the cell block. Parfitt picked up the bunch of cell keys without being asked and led the way into the cells. Monroe did not relax his alertness until Oakley was safely behind bars.

'I saw Mattie out at the Denton place,' Monroe told Twitchell. 'She'll be safe while Bud Hanna is alive. I'm going back out there now to try and get her away from the gang. I came back to get the two men Hanna sent in. If I can split the gang and take them one by one, I've got a good chance of beating this set-up.'

'I'll go with you,' Twitchell said. 'Two guns are better than one.'

'No. I can handle this better alone. Stay here, Doc. I know it's hard for you, but you've got to give Mattie as much chance as you can. I've heard some terrible stories about Mack Hanna. He's a mad dog.'

'I'm counting on you, Wes.' Twitchell sighed help-lessly. 'Don't let anything bad happen to Mattie.'

'What happened to that wounded drover?' Monroe asked.

'I treated him, and his pards took him back to their camp.'

'What are Bud Hanna's chances of surviving the move from your place?'

'I think he'll be dead by morning.' Twitchell paced the office. 'I should have listened to you in the first place and had him transferred to the jail. Mattie would still be here if I had.'

'I'm usually right,' Monroe replied tersely.

He departed, filled with the desire to do something constructive, but aware that it would be difficult to rescue Mattie Twitchell from Mack Hanna's clutches. He headed back to the barn for his horse, his confidence down to its lowest ebb.

Mack Hanna was equally low in spirits. He paced around the camp-fire behind the Denton place while he wrestled mentally with his problems, watched by his remaining men. He no longer trusted Jack Thompson, and wondered if the man was playing a double game. He glanced at the intent faces watching him.

'Ike, I got a job for you. Go back to town and watch Thompson and Oakley. See what they get up to. They went in to kill that deputy. If they haven't done it by the time you get there, then do the job yourself, and if Thompson is nosing round the woman who keeps the dress shop instead of doing what I've told him, then put a slug in his back.'

Ike Cossey got to his feet. He was a big, wide-shouldered killer, with staring blue eyes. His teeth gleamed in the firelight.

'I'm on my way, Mack.' He went to the picket line and prepared his horse for travel.

'If Thompson is doing what I told him to, then leave him alone,' Hanna called.

'Sure thing,' Cossey replied.

'And in that case you can go to the dress shop, grab the girl, and bring her back here.'

'OK.' Cossey grinned. 'No sweat.'

Hanna stood watching until Cossey had ridden out, then went to the back of the wagon and climbed in. Mrs Twitchell was inside, crouching beside the stretcher on which Bud Hanna was lying. Wiley Carter was sitting in a corner, half-asleep, and Hanna kicked the man's feet, jerking him awake.

'Get out of here, Wiley,' Hanna rasped, and Carter sprang up, cursing, and departed muttering under his breath.

Hanna stood with his head bent under the canvas top, his shadow grotesquely distorted by the lantern which threw dim light over the interior of the wagon. Mattie Twitchell was on her knees beside the wounded man. She had opened Bud's shirt to bare the blood-stained bandage around his chest.

Bud's eyes were open and he was trying desperately to speak, but could only emit a whining moan.

'He's lucky,' observed Mrs Twitchell. 'The wound hasn't opened.'

'Does that mean he'll be OK?'

'It doesn't mean any such thing.' Mattie's dark eyes glittered in the lamplight when she looked up at the gang boss. 'I can't be sure of anything. Your father is old, and he's lost a lot of blood. You were advised not to move him, but he's been bumped along in this wagon for almost an hour. If I didn't know better, I would think you wished to kill him. As it is, I think it will be touch and go. The least you should have done was brought my husband along instead of me. He's the doctor. I'm only a nurse. I can only watch, I'm afraid. There's little I can do beyond praying.'

'Praying? Is he that bad? Heck, he's had worse wounds than this one and pulled through.'

'Maybe, when he was younger, but he's an old man now.'

Mack Hanna bent over the stretcher and looked into his father's eyes. Bud was conscious. He looked feverish. His eyes blinked and his mouth opened, his lips trying to frame words.

'Pa,' Mack said softly, 'don't try to talk. You're gonna be all right. Try to sleep. I'll get the doctor back to you in the morning.'

'I'm good as dead, Mack.' Bud's voice was low-pitched and hesitant. 'You better leave me to die in peace and get the hell out of here.'

'You ain't gonna die, Pa. You're on the mend now. The doc did a good job on you. I ain't gonna let you die.'

Bud Hanna shook his head and closed his eyes, seeming to shrink into himself. His breathing was harsh, rasping through the silence, each successive respiration sounding like it would the last. Mack Hanna straightened, his face betraying unaccustomed emotion. He was appalled by his father's condition, and angered by the inevitability confronting him.

'By God, he better live!' He spoke furiously. 'If he dies, I'll kill every man, woman and child in that town, and wipe the place off the face of the earth, so help me.'

'His life is in the hands of the Lord,' Mrs Twitchell

said firmly, 'so it might be better not to blaspheme.'

Mack jumped down from the wagon. It was in him to go into town and grab the doctor. He stood by the camp-fire, his eyes glittering as he gazed into the leaping flames, his face ugly with desperation. Whatever the outcome of his father's condition, he promised himself, he would make Bitter Creek suffer when daylight came.

NINE

Monroe went to the spot near the stable where he had left his horse, and was tightening the girth preparatory to riding out, when he heard the sound of horses approaching along the trail. He moved to the front corner of the barn and peered from the shadows, wondering if Mack Hanna was returning. He saw riders coming, and was startled when four drovers appeared. They passed the stable and rode along the street, not looking left or right. Monroe left the shelter of the barn and hurried along behind them, fearing more trouble.

The four dismounted outside the saloon and hitched their mounts to the rail. Monroe rushed to catch up, and reached the batwings after the men had passed inside. He peered in over the swing doors and saw the four walking to the bar, behind which Pete Feeney was wiping glasses. Feeney looked up at the newcomers and stiffened. His right hand dropped out of sight below the bar as Monroe pushed through the batwings and entered to halt on the threshold.

Two of the four drovers dropped their hands to their holsters and grasped their pistols. Feeney lifted a Colt from under the bar. Monroe palmed his gun ahead of them and cocked it.

'Hold it right there!' he called.

All eyes turned towards him, and action ceased. The two drovers had their weapons half-drawn. Feeney was pointing his gun across the bar, its hammer already cocked, but relief showed on his features when he saw Monroe.

'What's going on?' Monroe advanced a couple of steps towards the drovers.

'We've come in for a drink,' said one of them.

'After the trouble we got from your pards earlier, the town is off-limits to drovers.' Monroe spoke as if he were discussing the weather. The drovers gazed stolidly at him and his levelled gun. 'Get out of here and head back to the herd. Don't show your faces again unless you're looking for trouble.'

Feeney was resting his right elbow on top of the bar, his gun steady, pointing at the drovers. There was a fixed grin on his lips, and his eyes were glinting in the bright lamplight. Silence closed in, filled with raw tension, and the four men stood motionless while they considered the probabilities. With Monroe covering them from behind, they were well aware of the danger in their position.

'OK,' one of them said. 'Pull in your horns. We ain't likely to stay where we ain't wanted. We'll split the breeze.'

They came to the door in a tight group, hands clear of weapons. Monroe stepped aside and they pushed through the batwings. Monroe followed them closely and stood on the sidewalk, his gun-hand down at his side, his pistol cocked. The four drovers climbed into the leather, turned their mounts, and rode out of town at a fast clip.

Monroe stood motionless until the sounds of their departure had faded. When silence returned, he uncocked his gun and eased it into his holster. He went back into the saloon and approached the bar.

'That was a close one,' Feeney observed. 'Sure, they were on the prod all right. You showed up at just the right time, Wes. A moment later and shooting would have started.'

'I was down by the livery barn when they came in, so I followed them along the street. I reckon you should close the place now, Pete, in case they come back.'

'I can't do that!' Feeney's eyes widened in horror. 'Teague would have my job off me, so he would.'

'Teague is not in a position to do anything. Stay open if you like, but I won't be around to help if those drovers decide to come back. I've got something else to worry about. The drovers seem mighty single-minded about nailing your hide to the barn door. You should get out of sight and stay clear until morning. I'm hoping things will be different around here by then.'

Feeney shook his head obstinately. 'It's more than my job is worth. I'll have to take my chances here.'

'OK. Just don't expect any help from me.' Monroe shrugged and departed.

He stood in the shadows on the sidewalk for several minutes, watching the street. The night seemed ominous. The darkness was dense, hostile, able to hide a watching man who could be waiting to kill Wes. Monroe drew a deep breath, held it as long as he could, then exhaled slowly, ridding himself of accumulated tension. He started along the sidewalk back to the livery bam, his hand close to the butt of his holstered gun.

'Wes.'

His name shivered out of the darkness of an alley and Monroe halted, his gun leaping into his hand.

'Hold it, Wes. It's me, Luke Baine.'

'Luke! What the hell are you trying to do, get yourself killed?'

'I need to talk to you, Wes, and I don't want to show myself. You can't handle this trouble alone, so I want you to know that I'm ready to back you if those outlaws come back.'

'That's kind of you, Luke.' Monroe was touched by the offer. 'Since when did you become a gunman?'

'Don't take that attitude, Wes. Me and some others have helped you out before.'

'Sure, and I'm always grateful to the townsmen for their public spirit, but this time it's different, Luke. Mack Hanna and his gang aren't ordinary criminals. Could you and the other townsmen fight off that gang if I were killed first?'

'Hell, no! But you *won't* be killed first, Wes.'

'Can you guarantee that?' Monroe smiled. 'Forget about it, Luke. If Hanna found out you were helping me, he'd have the town burned down around your ears before you could pull your gun. Thanks for the offer, but you'd better get off the street like the rest of the townsmen. It'll help me considerably if I don't have anyone getting under my feet. There's been hell to pay already this evening, and it ain't over yet, not by a long rope.'

'OK. I get your point.' Reluctance sounded in Baine's voice. 'But it goes against the grain to sit by while thugs rampage around the town.'

'You would have helped more if you'd stood your ground with the Town Council when I asked you to, and insisted that the law department should be reinforced by an extra deputy while Sam was laid up. It's too late now, Luke. The chips are down, and I have to play the cards I'm dealt with. Go home now and stay under cover.'

'Good luck then, Wes.' Baine's boots echoed in the alley as he departed.

Monroe went on along the sidewalk. A few moments later, the short hairs on his neck began tingling as some intangible sixth sense warned him that he was not alone in the darkness. He halted abruptly, palming his gun, his eyes narrowing to pierce the night. He felt certain someone had moved in close to him, though he saw and heard nothing. It was a sensation prompted by some primeval instinct. He stretched out his left hand to feel for the nearest wall, wanting to put his back against it. In the absence of sight, his ears were strained for the slightest sound.

He heard the scrape of leather on the sidewalk, saw a shapeless figure lean forward from deep shadow into the straying beam issuing from the nearest streetlamp, and caught a glint of light on the blade of a knife as it was hurled at him.

He twisted and lunged to the right, saving himself from getting the point of the knife dead centre. The razor-sharp blade struck him in the fleshy part of his upper left arm, slicing through thick flesh to the bone. Sickening pain sped along the length of the limb. He fell back against the wall and the knife was jarred out of the wound.

Intent on catching the assailant, Monroe leaned

forward, eyes narrowed to pick up a glimpse of the man, who had darted away almost before the knife reached its target. He heard boots on the sidewalk, but saw only a half-crouching figure running for cover. He threw up his gun and lined the weapon on the moving figure, but the man disappeared into an alley before he could fire.

Monroe ran to the alley, his gun ready, hearing the boots of the fleeing man rapping on the hard-packed dirt. He could see nothing, and fired three spaced shots along the length of the alley. When the echoes of the shooting faded, there was utter silence. His assailant had lost himself in the impenetrable darkness of the back lots.

Blood was running down Monroe's arm. He clenched his teeth against the pain that was invading the limb from shoulder to fingertips, and set off at a run along the alley. When he reached the far end he halted, breathing heavily, listening for sounds. There was nothing, and he paused to examine his wound. He was losing a lot of blood, so removed his neckerchief, wadded it into a ball, and thrust it inside his coat against the wound.

He heard the clatter of someone falling over a pile of empty cans, and started forward instantly. More clattering followed. Monroe knew exactly where the cans were, and hurried forward almost at a run despite the darkness, for he knew the area well. He reached the cans, paused again, ears strained, and heard boots thudding on hard ground. It sounded like a drunk making his way home, and Monroe fancied that one of his shots must have winged his assailant. He went on, discarding caution in his desire to catch the man.

A gun-flash tattered the shadows ahead, and he heard the crackle of a bullet passing his head. The crash of the shot hammered and threw echoes across the town. A dog began to bark frenziedly. Monroe returned fire instantly, aiming for the flash, and two shots sped on their way before his hammer struck an empty cartridge. He reloaded quickly, plucking shells from the loops on his cartridge belt, then paced forward. He heard a groan just ahead, and halted.

The night was too dark for him to see anything clearly, but he spotted a shapeless figure huddled on the ground, and moved in cautiously, his gun covering the figure. As he drew nearer, he saw a pistol lying on the ground, and picked up the gun, holstering his own weapon. When he bent over the figure, his fingers discovered that the man was dead.

Sitting back on his heels, Monroe glanced around into the darkness. The breeze moaned in his ears. He reached for a match and struck it, cupping it in his hands and holding it close to the upturned features. Shock stabbed him deeply when he recognized the face of one of the drovers whom he had sent out of town, for he had been expecting to find an outlaw. He extinguished the match and sat back on his heels. Those drovers were proving to be one hell of a problem.

The pain in his arm jarred through his musing, and he arose and went along the back lots to the alley beside the jail. When he entered the law office, he found Doc Twitchell still pacing up and down.

'I heard the shots,' Twitchell said. He spotted the blood on Monroe's left arm and took charge. 'Sit down on a corner of the desk, Wes. Was it one of the outlaws who did this?'

'I thought it was, until I nailed him, but it turned out to be a drover. He's lying dead on the back lots. I've got to get moving, Doc. I need to get back to the outlaws and start my move to wipe them out.'

'It's a clean wound. It'll need a couple of stitches. You won't be able to use the arm for some days, Wes, and you can't go up against those outlaws with only one good arm.'

'I can use a pistol one-handed. Don't give me a hard time, Doc. I got enough on my plate as it is.'

He suffered the doctor's treatment in silence, teeth clenched against the pain, his mind focused on what he had to do next. The pain merely sharpened his senses, brought home to him the extreme measures he would have to use to bring normality back to this town and its people. Life had become a nightmare from the moment he heard that Jack Thompson was returning.

He stood up when the doctor began to roll down the bloodstained sleeve over the heavily bandaged wound, thankful that the pain was easing.

'Thanks, Doc. I'll be on my way now.'

'Let me ride with you, Wes. I wouldn't get in your way. If you managed to get Mattie away from the outlaws, I could bring her back to town, and she wouldn't be on your hands if you had more fighting to do.'

'Nice try, Doc.' Monroe shook his head. 'I see it as a one-man job. It wouldn't be so good if I rescued Mattie then found you'd been killed in the shoot-out, huh?'

He stood up and moved his left arm experimentally. It seemed to be stiffening, but was easier than before Twitchell had started working on it. Leaving the office, he stood in the shadows for a moment, gathering his strength and his thoughts. He was being forced to waste time on side issues when he should be out there, confronting the outlaws. He needed to get Mattie Twitchell away from Mack Hanna before he could pit himself against the gang.

His arm was throbbing and hurting so much down at his side that he removed his neckerchief, fashioned a sling, and slipped the forearm into it, supporting it at an angle of forty-five degrees across his chest, which made the limb feel easier. He sighed with relief as he walked towards the livery barn.

He turned aside at the saloon and pushed through the batwings. Pete Feeney looked up from behind the bar. The bartender gazed at Monroe's injured arm and shook his head.

'Gimme a whiskey, Pete, and make it a big one.'

Feeney poured the drink and Monroe picked up the glass. He drank half its contents and replaced the glass on the bar.

'I needed that, but I better not drink it all. I got work to do.'

'Is it true those bank robbers took the wounded outlaw from Doc's place, Wes?'

Monroe nodded.

'And they took Mattie Twitchell to nurse him?' Feeney persisted.

'You got it, Pete. I'm on my way to put matters right. Stand the rest of my drink on the back of the bar. I'll be in for it when I get through.'

'Sure an' all, and shall I book a place for you on Boot Hill while I'm at it?'

'Luke Baine will have to dig several holes out there

before this business is done,' Monroe observed coldly, and departed.

He stood on the sidewalk and checked his gun. Then he was ready. He went to where he had left his horse, and swung into the saddle. It was then he heard the thin scream of a woman in trouble, and twisted in leather to look around. The scream sounded again, seeming to come from behind the barn.

Monroe turned his mount and drew his gun, sending the horse towards the rear of the stable. The next instant a rider came around the corner, heading for out of town, with a woman across the saddle who was fighting him all the way. Monroe thought he heard Sue's voice, and cold realization swept through him. The two horses almost collided. Monroe leaned forward and crashed his gun against the rider's head. The man groaned and ceased trying to subdue the woman. He fell sideways out of leather, and she dropped heavily to the ground.

Monroe grabbed the reins of the nervous horse and stepped down from his saddle, moving around to cover the man. The woman was getting to her feet, protesting loudly, and he was shocked when he found it *was* Sue. The rasp of metal against leather alerted him as the man on the ground drew his gun. He levelled his own weapon at the dark shape and fired two quick shots. The crash of the gun blasted his ears, and the flash half-blinded him. Then Sue was grasping his arm, pulling down his gun-hand.

'That's Jack Thompson!' she screamed.

TEN

Monroe stared at the motionless figure on the ground, his mind overwhelmed by shock. He turned his attention to Sue. She was sobbing, her face a pale blur in the night. He put his right arm around her shoulder, his gun dangling from his hand.

'Tell me what happened, Sue.'

'Oh, Wes, I came out of my shop when I heard the fighting. Jack had knocked you down and was set to shoot you. I told him I'd go away with him if he let you live, and he took me at my word. We went along the back lots to my home to get some of my clothes, and then came to the stable for his horse. I tried to get away from him, but he wouldn't let me go.'

'So he was taking you out of town.' Monroe bent over Thompson and checked him out. When he straightened, his face was stiff with shock. 'He's dead, Sue. What a damned fool he's been! He had everything three years ago, and threw it all away to ride with outlaws.'

A boot scraped beyond the corner of the barn as Monroe whirled, gun lifting.

'It's me, Luke Baine, Wes. What's going on?'

'It's OK, Luke. Here's another customer for you.'

Baine stepped into view, a pistol in his hand.

'Anyone I know?'

'Jack Thompson.' Monroe felt as if a cloud lifted from his mind as he answered. 'Take care of Sue, Luke. She's had a bad shock. I have to leave town now. I've wasted too much time as it is.'

'My wife will look after Sue. Maybe I can ride with you now, huh?'

'The answer is still no.' Monroe patted Sue's shoulder. 'Go with Luke, honey. I'll see you when I get back. This bad business is just about over.'

He turned, caught up the trailing reins of his horse and swung into the saddle. A voice called to him from behind and he turned swiftly, recognizing Doc Twitchell's voice.

'I heard the shooting, Wes. Is there anything I can do?'

'Luke will tell you about it, Doc.'

Monroe set his heels against the flanks of his horse. The animal lunged forward and hit a fast pace out of town. Sue cried out as he was swallowed up in the night, but he did not understand what she said. He straightened in the saddle and let the horse run southwards, knowing exactly what he had to do. A showdown was waiting for him at the Denton place.

Monroe left the trail long before he reached the outlaw camp. The moon was riding high in the sky, showing intermittently through breaks in the cloud, which were being chivvied along by a strong breeze, like a herd of cattle crossing the range. He moved in a wide half-circle to reach a spot south of the derelict ranch, and left his horse in cover. As he paused to get his bearings, he suddenly gained the uncomfortable feeling that he was being watched. The hair prickled on the back of his neck and he dropped to the ground, snaking his pistol out of its holster as he did so and grimacing at the pain flaring in his left arm.

Monroe knew he could take no chances with the outlaws. They were savages, men who were ready to kill without compunction. He lay, watching his surroundings, ears strained for the slightest noise. Tense moments flitted by, and he was about to go on when he heard a twig snap under a furtive boot somewhere at his back. He waited with the patience that came from experience, his heart thudding painfully in his breast, and drew a long breath to disperse his tension.

A slowly moving figure suddenly materialized only yards away. Monroe figured the man for a guard circling the outlaw camp and remained still. The man came on. He was carrying a rifle, intent upon his duty, not taking any chances. He covered every angle of his surroundings as he moved, and for some moments Monroe thought he would be discovered, but the man passed by and went on into the shadows, hardly making a sound as he circled the silent camp.

Monroe considered the situation, estimating that Hanna had six men – too many to be tackled together. He needed to take them singly, if the opportunity arose, and he had to start with the guard. He arose immediately and moved after the flitting figure. Moments later, he saw the outline of the wagon behind the ruined shack. A dim light illuminated the interior of the wagon, but was not bright enough to penetrate the canvas top.

The moon was shining in a clear patch of sky, spreading a silvery light that made vision deceptive and heightened the shadows. The guard went into the camp, stirred a sleeping man with the toe of his boot, then moved on to his blankets and settled down. Monroe watched the second man rise, pick up his rifle and move off into the night. The camp remained silent and still.

Monroe dropped flat and crawled towards the wagon. The rear of the vehicle was pointed towards the camp only yards from where the outlaws were sleeping. The team had been unhitched and were knee-hobbled close by. One of the animals lifted its head and gazed in Monroe's direction, and he froze until it resumed grazing.

He reached the front of the wagon. A canvas drape had been pulled across the driving-seat to conceal the interior. Monroe stood up in the shadow of the wagon, gun in hand, and put his back to the vehicle. The silence was intense. He tried to find a hole in the canvas to get a glimpse of the interior, but found nothing. He expected Mattie Twitchell to be inside with the wounded man, and accepted that she would not be alone. One of the gang, probably Mack Hanna himself, would be inside, guarding her and keeping a check on Bud Hanna's condition.

Monroe put a foot on a front wheel of the wagon and stepped up off the ground. He felt the wagon move slightly under his weight and the springs creaked in protest. He froze, gun lifted ready for action, his breathing restrained as he awaited the inevitable reaction from inside. Moments passed slowly. When there was no challenge from the occupants, he began to breathe again. He reached out and, taking hold of the canvas drape, eased it aside an inch at a time until he could peer into the wagon.

Mattie Twitchell was huddled over a blanket-covered figure lying in the centre of the wagon-bed, and Monroe saw a man hunched in a corner of the wagon, supposedly on guard, but snoring softly.

Mrs Twitchell was not asleep. She sat by Bud Hanna's side, gazing intently at his composed face in the dim lamplight. Monroe paused to look around the silent camp. The guard was on the far side, making a patrol of the perimeter, and he wondered where Mack Hanna was. Then he eased aside the drape and stepped into the wagon. Mrs Twitchell gasped when she caught his movement, and looked up.

'Wes, what are you doing here?'

Monroe took three strides and passed her as the sleeping guard stirred and began to open his eyes. Monroe's pistol rose and fell. There was a dull thud of steel striking flesh and the guard subsided inertly.

'Come on,' Monroe urged in an undertone. 'I'll take you out of here. Hurry. We don't have much time.'

'I can't leave, Wes. I have to see this through. This man will be dead by morning, and I promised him I'd stay to the end. Hurry and get away yourself. They'll surely kill you if they catch you.'

'Come on, for the doc's sake!' Monroe grasped the woman's arm and pulled her to her feet. 'You owe Bud Hanna nothing. Doc wanted to come here with me. He was willing to risk his life to get you away, but I talked him out of it despite his determination, and he's waiting for you back in town. I promised him I'd get you out, so you'd better come away before it's too late.'

'I won't leave!' She gazed into Monroe's face. 'You're wasting your time, Wes. '

'I won't leave without you. If you stay, then so will I.' Monroe cocked his gun. He dropped to one knee, remaining silent and still. 'I'm ready to die doing my job,' he added softly, 'and I reckon Mack Hanna will be the first outlaw through that flap, which will suit me, because if I nail him the rest will quit.'

Mrs Twitchell sighed as she regarded Monroe, her eyes glinting in the soft lamplight. Then she arose and turned unsteadily, shaking her head as she climbed out over the driving-seat and descended to the ground. Monroe followed her quickly and led her away from the camp, keeping the wagon between them and the sleeping outlaws. He heaved a sigh of relief when they gained the shadows around the perimeter of the camp without arousing the badmen.

The guard was yards ahead, walking steadily, swinging in a wide circle around the sleeping camp. Monroe edged away to the right, eventually reaching the spot where he had left his horse. He checked for the guard, but the man had disappeared beyond a thicket. Monroe tightened his cinch and put the reins into Mrs Twitchell's hands.

'Walk him away from here for a good hundred yards before you get into the saddle,' he instructed. 'Do you know your way into town from here?'

'I do. I've lived around here for thirty years.'

'Good. Doc should be in the law office. Go there and set his mind at rest. I'll see you when I get back to town.'

'Thank you, Wes. I do appreciate what you're doing.'

'Sure. We'll talk about it some more when I get through out here.'

She departed, leading the horse, and Monroe stood

looking around until she had gone into the night. He heard the faint click of a hoof against a stone, then silence descended.

Monroe turned back to the camp, gun in hand. He had a good chance now of succeeding in his deadly chore, and the first thing he had to do was run off the horses. He was aware that the outlaws had picketed their mounts only yards away from where they were sleeping, and moved forward slowly, watching for the guard in case the man varied his route around the camp. He heard a horse whicker somewhere in the darkness and pinpointed the direction.

As he sighted the wagon again, the man he had knocked senseless inside it came leaping out, shouting to awaken the camp.

'Hey, wake up! The woman's gone. She hit me and laid me out.'

Sleeping figures became animated, and Mack Hanna, who had not been sleeping, appeared from the darkness beyond the camp.

'What happened, Farrell?' Hanna demanded. 'You must have been asleep if she got the chance to hit you.'

'I wasn't asleep. She hit me unexpected with something solid.'

Hanna climbed into the wagon to check the condition of his father, then jumped to the ground again.

'How's he doing?' Someone asked.

'Still alive. Move around and find that woman. Spread out and search. She can't get far on foot. Billy, you're on guard. Did you see or hear anything?'

'Nary a thing, Mack, or I would have stopped her. Mebbe she sprouted wings and flew back to town, huh?'

Monroe faded back into deeper shadow as the half-dozen men turned to search the immediate area of the camp. Hanna stood at the back of the wagon, looking around, an ominous black figure in the night. Monroe crouched in the shadows, waiting and watching, aware that he could do nothing until this present alarm was over.

A horse snickered again, and the sound came from Monroe's right. He started in that direction, watching Hanna and half-expecting the gang boss to check on the picketed animals, but Hanna did not move. Monroe saw moonlight glint on the weapon the gang boss was holding, and eased away to find the horses.

Monroe found seven horses tied to a single rope stretched between two trees. He looked around for the guard. None of the outlaws, spread out in the search for Mrs Twitchell, was close to the camp, and most of them had set off towards town, expecting the woman to head in that direction.

Monroe closed in on the horses. He had started to untie the nearest horse when his keen ears caught the sound of approaching hoofs coming from the direction of Bitter Creek. He froze, listening intently, hoping that Mattie Twitchell was not coming back. He eased into the thicket beyond the horses and watched the camp.

The incoming rider was suddenly accosted by one of the searching outlaws. A hoarse voice called a challenge, and almost immediately a gun blasted, throwing a string of harsh echoes through the night. The approaching hoofs stopped. Hanna started away from the wagon, making for the scene of the disturbance. Monroe edged along in cover, keeping Hanna in sight.

'What in hell is going on?' Hanna demanded hoarsely.

'Rider came in,' someone replied from the shadows. 'I told him to halt, but he tried to ride me down.'

'Did you kill him?' Hanna demanded.

'Nope. It's that doctor from town. There ain't no fight in him. He wants his wife back, that's all.'

Monroe compressed his lips at the news. Twitchell had finally lost his patience, and it was ironic that he had placed himself in Hanna's hands when his wife was on her way back to town.

'So, you want your wife, huh?' Hanna remarked to Doc Twitchell. 'Well, you can't have her.'

'What have you done to her?' The doctor stood straight and defiant, completely unafraid, although he was aware that he was facing death at the hands of these men. 'I'll kill you if you've harmed her. You don't need her here now I've shown up. Send her back to town on my horse, and I'll take care of your father – if you haven't killed him already by moving him out of town.'

'Your wife ain't here.' Hanna chuckled. 'She fooled one of my men and escaped. I got the men out searching for her. But now you're here, you can look in on my pa. Get up in the wagon and stay there. Someone will be watching you, and you'll collect a slug if you so much as stick your nose outside.'

'Do you swear that my wife is unharmed?' Twitchell demanded.

'I told you, didn't I? Get into that wagon before I lose my patience.'

The doctor obeyed and Hanna accompanied him. Monroe turned away to go back to the horses, aware that he could use the doctor's arrival to his advantage. He untied the horses, waved his arms, and set them moving away from the camp. When they were jostling away together, he fired a shot into the air behind them, and they streamed off into the night.

Yells came from all over the area as the sound of pounding hoofs carried through the shadows. Monroe moved out swiftly, seeking cover, and dropped behind a large rock. He saw the outlaws beginning to return to the camp, and shouted a warning that halted them in their tracks.

'This is the law,' he called. 'I've got you surrounded. Drop your guns and surrender.'

He did not expect the outlaws to obey, but wanted them to know that the law had caught up with them. He ducked when guns hammered and flashes split the night. Slugs came whining around the rock, splattering against it and ricocheting noisily. Monroe opened fire with his pistol, aiming for gun-flashes, and the shadows were tattered by the furious shooting, the darkness impossible to penetrate between the alternating extremes of light and dark.

Monroe changed position quickly. He moved back and to the right, paused to reload his empty chambers, and fired again at the gun-flashes erupting in front of him. The racket of blasting guns hammered against his ears. He could tell by the gun-flashes that some of the outlaws were trying to move around him, and he increased his shooting, certain that he was scoring hits on the badmen. He dropped flat and waited for the action to calm down, and moments later an uneasy silence settled.

'Two of you men work your way around behind him,' Mack Hanna shouted. 'There ain't no posse out there, boys. It's one man doing the shooting. Get round there and kill him.'

Monroe eased back and moved to the left, half-circling the camp until he was opposite the wagon. He crouched and waited, and soon spotted a furtive figure moving around to outflank him. He aimed and squeezed his trigger. The man fell as if flattened by a giant hand. Monroe was already on the move when other guns fired at his position.

Being alone gave Monroe a distinct advantage. Anyone moving around in front of him had to be an outlaw. He crawled in closer to the wagon, his eyes narrowed as he probed the shadows for Mack Hanna's big figure. He did not think the gang boss would move far from his father's side. Two of the outlaws were shouting, way out to the left. They had reached a cut-off position behind Monroe's original vantage-point and were reporting to Hanna that they could not locate the lawman. Monroe bared his teeth in a mirthless grin. He was happy with the situation. Out here, clear of town, only the badmen and himself could suffer the consequences of this action.

He saw a faint movement beside the wagon and lifted his gun. Hanna was his prime target. If he nailed the outlaw boss, the others would soon quit, but he held his fire. A stray bullet striking the wagon would penetrate and probably kill Doc Twitchell or the wounded man inside. He saw a figure at the side of the wagon which dropped to the ground and crawled under the vehicle.

A furtive sound in the brush to his right warned Monroe that an outlaw was approaching. He half-turned to face the threat, and fired two quick shots when he spotted a figure sneaking towards him. He threw himself down almost before his bullets were in flight. The next instant, two guns opened fire at him from the left. Slugs crackled over his head and he rolled into fresh cover, clenching his teeth against the pain that surged through his left arm.

Two men came towards him at a run, firing swiftly. Monroe lifted his gun, drew a bead on the left-hand man, and squeezed his trigger. The outlaw was blown away as if by a strong wind. He moved again as the second man began to shoot at him, then fired quickly, sending two slugs into the centre of the moving shadow. As he rolled away, a gun flashed from beneath the wagon and a bullet struck his left arm, just above the elbow.

Pain flared through Monroe's already-damaged limb. He dropped to the ground, losing his gun, and rolled on to his back to check his arm. Fresh pain was flaring through it from fingers to shoulder. He found blood oozing from a wound just below the bicep. He looked around. Yet another outlaw was coming towards him, and he scrabbled on the ground for his gun. His fingers touched the hot weapon. He snatched it up and fired a shot, then the hammer clicked on a spent cartridge. He clawed fresh shells from the loops on his belt and thumbed them into the smoking weapon.

Monroe's ears were filled with gun thunder, and the reek of burned powder was strong in his nostrils. The pain in his left arm was becoming intolerable. He gritted his teeth and forced himself to go on, keeping low, his gun uplifted. Now the silence was intense and there was no way of knowing how many of the outlaws were still in action. He needed to change his position, but was aware that to do so would betray him to the outlaws.

A gun flashed over by the wagon. Monroe ducked as the slug passed dangerously close to his head. The pistol threw lead towards him in a continuous stream. Bullets whined around Monroe's elusive figure, slicing through trees and smacking against rocks in their blind flight. He returned fire while changing position, but as he showed himself above his cover, a bullet from beneath the wagon hit him in the left side, just below the ribs.

The impact thrust Monroe around. His gun fell from his hand. He tried to retain his balance, but swayed and sprawled, tottering as if he had been struck by a giant hammer. He fell heavily, white-hot pain searing through his body. His breath was forced out of his lungs by the agony and he gasped, pressing his right hand against the wound in a desperate attempt to assuage the pain striking through him.

The shooting had stopped. Monroe lay motionless, fighting shock, unable to do more than gasp helplessly. Then the initial pain of the wound eased and he moved slightly, wanting to find his gun. He thrust the inside of his left elbow against the bullet wound under his ribs and held it there tightly while he scrabbled for his pistol.

He found the weapon and scooped it up, jamming the hot muzzle between his left elbow and his body as he reloaded awkwardly. His senses were slipping in and out of consciousness. There was a loud ringing sound in his ears, and his sense of balance was affected. A series of flashing lights shimmered before his eyes, and he fell on his face in the shadows. His strength ebbed quickly and he could do no more than roll on to his back, gripping his gun desperately. As he began to lose consciousness, he heard the sound of boots thumping the hard ground, coming towards him from his right, and he struggled against the inevitable.

Monroe was filled with desperation, aware that if he gave in to his weakness he would die. He fought against the blackness that seemed to spring up around him on all sides. Blinking against the desire to close his eyes and lose his hold on reality, he forced up his gun-hand and levelled the pistol as the nearing figure took shape before him.

His vision was behaving oddly, he was having trouble focusing, and complete darkness began to overwhelm his sight. He was racked with pain. He had fallen head-long and his face had struck the hard ground, yet he fought against his problems and held his gun steady, determined to finish the job he had set out to do.

'Declare yourself,' Monroe called in a clipped tone.

'Who do you think it is? I'm Mack Hanna, and I'm closing this game.'

A gun flamed and hammered. Monroe returned fire instinctively, aiming for the figure wavering before him. He heard the strike of a bullet hitting the ground a scant inch from him and closed his eyes against the flash of his own weapon as it bucked against the heel of his hand. Blackness descended upon him and he struggled against insensibility. He jerked his head upwards and his sight returned. When he looked around for Hanna, all he saw was a figure running back towards the wagon.

A sense of failure enveloped Monroe and he lowered his gun. He was lying flat on his back and found himself gazing up at the night sky. The moon was shining remotely. Clouds were racing across its pale yellow orb. The breeze was keen. Monroe sighed heavily and lost consciousness.

He lay as if dead for a long time, bloodied but not defeated, his pistol still clasped in his hand. Then his senses returned and he opened his eyes. At first he could do no more than blink at the moon, and when he finally attempted to move he was swamped with pain as his wounds protested. He rolled over to his right side, gathered his strength, then moved on to his face. He managed to get one knee under his body and pushed hard with his right arm, levering himself up from the ground.

When he was on hands and knees, he looked around. The wagon was opposite across the campsite, seemingly deserted, and he wondered what had happened to Doc Twitchell. He forced himself to his feet, teeth clenched against the pain coursing through his left side. Once erect he stood swaying, then staggered to a tree and slumped against it for support. He was still holding his gun and checked it, looking around for trouble.

He could see bodies scattered around the camp, and suddenly spotted movement off to the right. A figure was coming forward, and Monroe watched it pause beside one of the fallen outlaws. The man dropped to one knee and examined the outlaw. Monroe narrowed his eyes and waited, his pistol ready.

'Go more to the right,' a harsh voice shouted from the wagon. 'That deputy was twenty yards ahead of where you are now.'

Monroe tensed, recognizing Mack Hanna's voice.

'I've found only dead outlaws,' Doc Twitchell replied.

'Well, he's out there, and he must be dead or bad hurt, or he'd still be fighting. Find him, Doc. I wanta know where he is before I move again.'

Monroe gazed at the wagon, but was unable to see anything in the dense shadows. He lifted his gun, but held his fire, wanting Twitchell to come closer. He narrowed his eyes and watched the doctor's progress towards him.

'I'm here, Doc,' Monroe called in an undertone when Twitchell bent over an outlaw barely ten feet away. 'What's going on?'

'Wes.' Doc Twitchell came to Monroe's side and knelt down. 'Don't shoot at the wagon. Hanna's got Mattie. She came back here when she heard the shooting.'

Monroe cursed under his breath.

'Doc, remember I got my gun on your wife,' Hanna shouted. 'What are you doing over there? You better find that deputy, or I'll kill her.'

'Tell him I'm dead,' Monroe said.

'I've found him,' Twitchell shouted. 'He's dead.' He lowered his voice. 'Most of the outlaws are dead – just a couple of them bad wounded. Bud Hanna died in the wagon around the time you started shooting. You hit Mack Hanna in the chest, but it ain't serious. We need to get Mattie away from him, Wes.'

'Hey, Doc, if he's dead, then drag him out of cover where I can see him,' Hanna called.

'Do it,' Monroe said. 'If we can get him clear of the wagon, I can nail him. Drag me out, and don't get between me and the wagon.'

Twitchell grasped Monroe under the arms and dragged him forward into the camp. He dropped Monroe some ten yards from the wagon. Monroe lay with his right hand against his hip, his gun covering the wagon. His eyes were unable to pierce the shadows around the vehicle and he waited, summoning up the last dregs of his patience and strength.

'I can't drag him any more,' Twitchell called. 'Turn my wife loose so I can take her back to town.'

There was movement under the wagon and Monroe squinted his eyes. The next instant Mattie Twitchell came running towards her husband, and Monroe gritted his teeth because she was directly between Hanna and himself. Then the gang boss came out of cover.

'Round me up a horse, Doc,' he called, 'and I'll pull out of here. I got my gun on your wife, so you better do like I say.'

Twitchell grasped his wife and pulled her to one side. Monroe pushed his gun forward and triggered the weapon at the indistinct figure in front of the wagon. He fired two shots and Hanna went down as if his legs had been kicked from under him. Gun echoes drifted. Monroe watched Hanna intently, but the gang boss did not move.

Monroe dropped his gun and relaxed. As far as he could tell, the job was finished. He could feel his senses receding and tried vainly to hang on, but slipped away from reality despite his efforts. His senses fled, and he was conscious of relief as he surrendered to his wounds and relinquished his responsibility.

Doc Twitchell came to Monroe's side and examined him, then sighed and sat back on his heels.

'I need some help here, Mattie,' he called. 'We can save Wes if we work fast.'

Mattie Twitchell fetched the lantern out of the wagon and came to her husband's side. She dropped to her knees without comment and together they began

159

patching up Monroe. It was an hour before Twitchell decided that it would be safe to take the unconscious deputy back to town for further treatment. They loaded him into the wagon and moved out, leaving the dead outlaws strewn around the deserted shack and carrying the blissfully unaware Monroe back to the land of the living.